F
COA
COATSWORTH, ELIZABETH JANE
Door to the north

cp. 2

DATE DUE		
GAYLORD M-2		PRINTED IN U.S.A.

186

DOOR TO THE NORTH

A Saga ~~of Early~~ America

DOOR TO
THE NORTH

By ELIZABETH COATSWORTH

Illustrated by Frederick T. Chapman

~~~~~~~~~~~~~~~~~~~~~~~~~~~~~~~

HOLT, RINEHART AND WINSTON

New York ★ Chicago ★ San Francisco

PUBLISHED, *October*, 1950

SECOND PRINTING, *April*, 1951

THIRD PRINTING, *November*, 1952

FOURTH PRINTING, *April*, 1956

FIFTH PRINTING, *August*, 1958

SIXTH PRINTING, *November*, 1960

SEVENTH PRINTING, *November*, 1962

91481–0212

Printed in the United States of America

LAND OF THE FREE SERIES
Edited by ERICK BERRY

OTHER BOOKS BY ELIZABETH COATSWORTH

HERE I STAY

SWORD OF THE WILDERNESS

TALES OF THE GAUCHOS (Editor)

THE CAPTAIN'S DAUGHTER

THE CAT WHO WENT TO HEAVEN

THIEF ISLAND

FOR MORTON TERRY
*who carries on a dearly loved name
into the future*

CONTENTS

DOOR TO THE NORTH

Chapter 1

The King's House

THE SPRING of 1360 came early.

The weather had been warm for an April week,
and Paul Knutson, walking down the great hall
of the king's house, left behind him the damp track of
his shoes, wet from the streams that were bright as
quicksilver across the old snow of the Bergen streets.
He was still wearing his riding cloak, but under it, he
had put on a long red robe and a belt of carved walrus
ivory. There was no trace of his old limp, but he held

his heavy lion's head even higher than usual and looked about him at the king's people with a kind of insolence. Although he had always been a loyal king's man in the long troubles which Magnus had entered into with his Norwegian nobles, there were too many Swedes about the place for Paul Knutson's taste.

King Magnus Eirikson might be Norwegian on his mother's side, but it was his Swedish half that was turned toward the sun, and there flourished the Swedes of Gothland. Now as he sat in the carved high seat at the end of the hall, playing chess with Nicolas Byrgeson, he was surrounded by his Swedish attendants. There were not half a dozen Norsemen among them. It was an old dish to Paul Knutson, but it still had a bitter taste. He was not at home here. Yet where another man might have walked warily, he moved with arrogance toward the king, exchanging greetings with his acquaintances as he went, and looking at everyone from challenging blue eyes.

By the raised hearth in the corner of the room sat the queen and her ladies, busy over their endless embroideries. He saw his wife among them and thought he caught a glimpse of his daughter Ingrid's pale hair. They had wasted no time. The pages, as usual, seemed drawn toward where the maidens might be found. He knew most of them, or could guess their fathers from their faces and bearing. But there was one who stood by himself against a wall hanging of leaves and small animals. There was nothing to call attention to his tall, lean, young figure except an air of unhappiness or ill fortune about it. His page's clothes were neat; he held himself straight; he might, with his brooding face, have been merely thinking up some new boy's escapade; yet no one but guessed that he stood deep in some well of misfortune. When he glanced up at Paul Knutson, passing within six feet of him, he did not seem to see him. His eyes were extraordinary in that northern world, for they were nearly black under black brows, although his hair was fair enough. People had called him Olav Blackbrows sometimes, but Paul Knutson, startled by that black blind stare, exclaimed to himself, "What! King Magnus still keeps the coward's son about him? I thought he would have been sent home long before this! I wish I had not brought Ingrid here."

Even so, he had an impulse to stop to speak with the boy. If there had been any recognition in the eyes that brushed his face, he would in all decency have said something. But there was none. He might have been a tree or a stone, for all the life that came into Olav's eyes. "Well, well," thought Paul soberly. "Whatever we have been to each other, we are strangers now," and once again the sharp physical pain struck through him as he remembered Olav's father, Sigurd Olavson, once his sworn friend and honored of all men.

But the king had seen him and had pushed away the table on which he had been playing, so that the chessmen were thrown over, and Nicolas Byrgeson had risen, his small monkey's face eager with welcome. He said something to the king, whose hand went to the broad cross he wore at his neck, and he too looked eagerly toward Paul Knutson, now mending his pace toward them. Paul saw that whatever the business might be, Nicolas was at the bottom of it. Since his son had been killed by a falling horse, and his wife had left him, he had become deeply religious. People called him the King's Conscience.

"Are they planning between them another campaign to Christianize the Russians?" Paul wondered. "After

the tales we've heard of the black death in Russia,
surely our people won't follow them. Haven't we had
our bellyful of the plague here at home? Whatever
Magnus may urge, I'll not take a step toward Russia,
and that I swear by all the holy saints."

Obstinacy and pleasure struggled across Paul Knutson's face as the king took him by the hand and clapped
his shoulder warmly. They were men of an age, with
grown children, but still in their full vigor. They had
known one another, and, in the main, trusted one another for twenty years now, twenty years of foreign
wars and civil outbreaks and plague, yet good years,
too.

Many who had followed the old king faithfully had
broken with his grandson, but Paul could look Magnus
Eirikson in the face without shame. He had been faithful
to him in word and deed, and he had been rewarded by
being made warden of the northern provinces, and
lawman at the meeting of the people. Now Magnus
spoke to him with open affection.

"And how is my Paul?" he asked. "Never was man
more welcome to me than are you this day. Sit down,
sit down! Bring ale, someone. Nicolas, you must sit
with us while I explain the business. Now first tell me
why you think I sent for you?"

Paul's face, which had become open and frank, clouded, and he said warily, "Perhaps Russia, my lord?"

The king smiled.

"And if it were Russia?"

"I would not go."

The king laughed, but without amusement.

"There speaks a good Norwegian," he said impatiently. "No, no, Paul Knutson, this matter does not
concern Russia. Turn your thoughts from the east,

man, westward—westward as far as the mind can reach.
Now what do you see?"

"Iceland?"

"Oh, stretch! You have not sailed far enough."

"Greenland?"

"Yes, Greenland and beyond. Vinland, and who
knows where the world may end? But if they go beyond
the world, even so we must find them and bring them
back to Christ."

"My lord, you speak darkly, like an old rune. I do
not follow your meaning."

"Wait, my lord, let me explain to Paul," interrupted
Nicolas Byrgeson, thrusting his small ugly head forward
like a sheep getting to its feet. "The matter would be
clearer, Paul, if you had been here when the ship arrived
from Greenland. You haven't heard of it yet? It was
the talk of all Bergen. You did not linger at your inn,
I see, but came here directly as soon as you arrived."

"Ever faithful," put in Magnus, whose flow of ill
humor had abated.

Nicolas paid no attention to the king. His face looked
smaller and more lined than ever in his earnestness, his
small eyes sparkled like bits of mica in a seamed rock,
and his words rushed out over one another like sheep
driven by a rough dog down a narrow lane.

"It was a great thing, Paul," he went on, "the first
time in our lives that a ship has come from Greenland.
The men! the boat! but first the ship. It was a thing to
wonder at; yet, seeing it, my eyes were filled with tears.
No proper beams, the wood was driftwood, and only
the Lord in heaven knows how long it had been tossed
about in the seas, or from what lost shores it had floated.
They had carved a prow ornament of a walrus with
real tusks, and that was a fine sight. But, man, there

were almost no nails in her; only a few which they had
secured from a stranded ship found on the eastern
uninhabited shore, with skeletons in a cove above it.
They burned the keel there and took the iron and
brought back the bones to be buried in Christian soil.
But for the rest, instead of nails, they had used pegs of
wood and withies to strengthen her. You would not have
believed that such a ship could live a day among the
waves, yet they had come from Greenland to Iceland,
and from Iceland here."

He paused, swallowed painfully, and said in a low
voice: "I see the hand of God in it."

"Have they no iron, then, in Greenland?" Paul asked
with interest.

Magnus answered before Nicolas could speak.

"Yes, they say there is iron, but too little wood to
melt it. Arne, the last bishop, had his men burn bones
for fuel, but got little iron by that at Gardar. Truly, as
Nicolas has said, the ship was a moving sight. And they
had no anchor, even."

"But it was the men!" Nicolas broke in. "The men
more than the ship. There were seventeen of them,
dressed in frieze of their women's spinning. I am called
a little troll of a man—no, do not deny it—but I was tall
among these Greenlanders. And in their mouths, our
language had changed so that they seemed like strangers
who have but half-learned our speech. Not that the outer
case of a man matters. It is the soul that counts."

"And their souls are in peril," Magnus said quietly,
his hand again on the gold cross he wore. "They have
had, for a long time, no wine or bread for the sacrament. Only the dish upon which the consecrated host
was once laid is still shown to them, and their Com-
munion is but to gaze upon it. Those are my people,

and before heaven, I should be held to account if this
were to go on."

"You have still, my lord, the Knarr, the royal trading
vessel which in former times sailed to Greenland,"
Paul said reasonably. "What is to prevent your sending
it out again with hogsheads of wine and bushels of grain
for these people?"

"There speaks the cautious Norseman!" exclaimed
one of the bodyguard, who had been leaning against
the carved back of the high seat, listening over the king's
shoulder.

Paul shot him a frowning look.

"A Norseman will go wherever a Swede will, and
lead him there, Orm Karlsson!"

"Indeed that remains to be seen," replied the other
negligently, smoothing the sleeve of his brocaded robe.

"Friends! Friends!" cried Magnus. "No more of this,
I beg you. No man questions the courage of Norwegians
or of Swedes in this gathering. What Paul has said is
quite right, if it were only a matter of wine and bread.
But go on, go on, Nicolas, tell him what they told us."

Nicolas dipped his finger in the horn of ale he held
and made a wet tracing on the table before them.

"See, Paul, there is the island as we know it. No man
knows how it ends in the north. Some say it is indeed
joined to Norway and that Hall and his goat made
their way by foot over countless mountains, the animal
feeding on the grass between the glaciers. But most men
think that this is a tale to tell before the fire. Here, then,
is what we know. Here is the eastern coast, surrounded
winter and summer by a pack of ice, and inhabited
only by a few outlaws with a price on their heads. Here
is the cape to the south and, rounding that, you approach a harbor and the houses of men, and the

beginning of the Eastern Settlement, which is called by that name because it is east of the second settlement, though both are on the west coast. There are one hundred and ninety farmsteads along that shore and twelve churches, and many fiords where the grass grows green."

"So I have heard, Nicolas, since I was a child," exclaimed Paul with scarcely concealed impatience.

The little man smiled. "And what do you know, then, of the Western Settlement?"

"It is said to have some ninety farmsteads and four churches," Paul answered, still impatiently, "shorter summers, less grass. It is six days rowing in a six-man boat from the Eastern Settlement, I have heard."

"And men have lived there for three hundred and fifty years, men of our race," Magnus said softly. "And ever since Leif the Lucky brought the faith to Greenland, the church bells have rung out over the fields and fiords, and the wild creatures of the sea and ice have wondered at the sound. And now, now, my Paul!" Suddenly the king sprang to his feet, striking the table before him. "And now, there *is* no Western Settlement. Your learning is bitterly at fault!"

A kind of sigh ran through the room. Paul Knutson's face had whitened. "My lord, who has done this thing?"

Until now he had held himself a little aloof, a Norwegian among Swedes, but now he had forgotten such rivalries. He too was on his feet facing the king, leaning forward, his clenched hands on the table, his mouth hard and straight.

"Let me know their names and I will follow them to the ends of the earth, and demand blood vengeance."

As Paul caught fire, the light seemed to go out of the king, and he sank back into the carved chair behind him.

"Ale," he said, almost fretfully. "More ale, Sigurd.

Paul, it is not so easy—it is more terrible than you realize. The soul is more than the body, man. If it were only their bodies, I should be at rest about them."

"So should not I be," Paul declared, still standing. "You are half Swede, my lord, but I am all Norse and these men were Norsemen."

"That is why I sent for you, of course," the king answered sharply. "It is Norse business first and foremost."

"And these men are, not were," Nicolas joined in. "So far as we know, they are still alive."

Paul turned his head, bewildered.

"I am in a maze," he exclaimed. "What is this, Nicolas Byrgeson? First you say that the Western Settlement has been destroyed and now that they are alive. I did not come to the king's house to be baited for your amusement."

"The settlement was not destroyed. It was deserted."

There was a silence. Paul's face changed again. Now he sat down and folded his hands before him.

"Tell," he said.

Everyone in the room had gathered about the three men; even the queen and her ladies had left the fire and their embroidery; even the black-eyed page had been drawn into that silent swarm that clustered about the table on which the crude ale-drawn outline of Greenland was drying on the pine board, sipped at by an early fly or two.

Magnus Eirikson was sunk in thought and did not speak. It was Nicolas, called the King's Conscience, who took up the tale.

"There is a priest at Gardar in Greenland, a Norseman called Ivar Bardson, sent out from Norway some years ago. Someone brought a letter from him. When a

boatload of hunters returned saying that they had
passed by the Western Settlement, but had seen no
smoke rising from any of the farmsteads, it was he who
headed an expedition sent from the Eastern Settlement.
In these last years, the Skraelings, a small dark people
who move in skin boats, and dress in fur, like animals,
have been drawing nearer and nearer to the settlement,
and there has been trouble on the hunting grounds
between them and our people, so the Eastern Settlement was uneasy. Ivar Bardson took twenty men and
rowed up the coast for six days—as you so well remembered, Paul. And when he came to the Western Settlement, the houses were all there and the cows and sheep
and goats were grazing on the hill slopes, and a dog ran
down to the beach to meet them. But there was no fire
on any hearth, nor any boat in the boathouses, nor any
bell in the churches.

"Ivar found no one, living or dead, in or out of the
houses, though he went even to the remote farmsteads
on the lakes under the mountains. All were empty."

"And the Skraelings?"

"There was no sign of them, save perhaps of their
fires and circles of stones where their tents may have
stood near the beaches. Some of the men who had met
with them in the north believed that the Skraelings had
been there, but there were no new graves, either of
Skraelings or of Christian men, no burned houses—no,
not even an upset chair or a broken pot on the floor."

"They went away?"

"Yes, they must have gone away. And that summer
too. For the cattle cannot live through a winter there,
outside the barns, any more than here with us—even
less, perhaps. At any rate, there was no doubt that what
had happened had happened that summer."

"Why had they gone, then? If they went freely, without violence, what concern is that to us who never saw them?"

Nicolas looked sternly at Paul.

"Have you forgotten that we talked of souls? Now I fear that you are thin iron that takes heat quickly and then cools off in half an hour."

Paul Knutson's face, under its shock of yellow hair, flushed red.

"I am a man of action, Nicolas Byrgeson, not a clerk, adept with so many words. It seems to me that you spin out the matter, turning it this way and that. Tell me plainly what happened at the Western Settlement, and what is the king's will in the matter, and why I was sent for, and I will give you a plain answer. But I am not a boy to be praised and reproved by men who have never seen half the battles I have fought."

"If you speak of the king, he fought in Russia like an archangel!" shouted a courtier.

"You haughty fool!" cried another angrily, elbowing his way toward where Paul sat unmoved.

But Magnus awoke from his reverie.

"Peace! Peace!" he exclaimed. "Must I always live in the sound of brawling? Paul Knutson is right. He shall know the answer to his questions and without more words. Sigurd, give me that which is beneath the table."

When the page had handed him the object, the king leaned forward and placed it in Paul's hands, in complete silence, while everyone stood on tiptoe, leaning over his fellow's shoulder to see what the thing might be which answered the riddle of Greenland.

Paul sat with it held between his strong square hands. At first he saw only that it was a soapstone bowl, well shaped, with very thin sides, and an interlacing ornament along the rim which ended in eagle-headed handles. It was a pretty thing, but there was no answer here.

He frowned, turning it round and round, suspicious again lest he was somehow being made a fool of. Then, suddenly, Paul's hands grew still, and his brows drew together as he stared fixedly at a design lightly incised into the curve of the bowl. The object represented was common enough in every household, but it was one whose form had not appeared openly in Norway for more than three hundred years as seal or symbol. Yet Paul Knutson recognized it, and a shiver of something between fear and horror ran through him at the sight. Almost as though an evil might flow into his veins from the bowl he held, he put it quickly on the table and crossed himself.

Magnus Eirikson laughed with sudden harshness.

"Yes, my Paul, now you understand. The people of the Western Settlement have turned away from Christ. They have sought another home, somewhere, perhaps with the pagan Skraelings. Instead of the cross, they have turned to the hammer of Thor!"

Nicolas again was on his feet. His eyes had rolled back into his head so that the whites showed wide and startling under the iris, and his body was shaken like the body of a dog with the fits.

"Follow them, Paul Knutson," and his voice rose almost to a shriek. "Follow them as a hound follows the stag, as a weasel pursues the hare. Hunt them, sniff them out, dig them forth from their lairs, even if they have hidden themselves over the edge of the world. Never turn back while there is life in you. This is the quest for which the king has summoned you."

Chapter 2

Olav Sigurdson

THERE WAS NO TALK that day of dinner in the king's house. For hour after hour the plans went on, and a priest made notes on parchment of the things which were needed: forty men, as many as the king's trading ship would carry; new sails, two new stern boats with oars and sails, extra swords, axes, spears, fur-lined cloaks, boots, new casks for water for the voyage; wine and ale, and grain, for Greenland; scythes, daggers, swords, cutlery of all sorts, fire steels, linen for church use, a little stained-glass window as a present to the Cathedral of St. Nicolas from Nicolas Byrgeson, timbers and wood, cloth and stoneware pitchers. The queen, Blanche of Namur, promised a fine French tapestry for the bishop's house at Gardar, and her ladies vied with one another in offering silver brooches and cloak clasps with which to buy a statue of the Virgin with the Child in her arms, to be set up in the cathedral or in one of the churches.

"And whoever will make presents of raisins, or dried apples or of nuts, or of sugar plums and cherries, may do so, for such things are rarely seen or tasted in Greenland and would be remembered half a man's life," said Magnus.

"I shall send my second-best dress so that the ladies may see what manner of clothes we wear here," cried one of the younger queen's women.

"And I, my cloak," "And I, my hood," "And I, my mantle," "And I, my pointed shoes," the others took up.

Not to be outdone, one of the younger dandies, Benedikt Karlsson, brother of the Orm who had jeered at Paul that morning, offered to send his pale blue cap and French surcoat to show the men of Greenland what the fashions were at court.

"We laugh," said the king, "and laughter is a good thing. It is time for the tables to be brought in and for us to eat and drink. But remember that this voyage is a true crusade. The Pope had authorized us to make a crusade against the Russians, but God willed that the black death should ride there in our stead. Just as I asked my soul if there were some fault in me that the Lord held back my hand from his service, he sent instead these seventeen men from Greenland that I might know that he still had use for me."

He turned to Paul with a sudden boyish and charming smile.

"And for you, my Paul," he added, clapping him on

the shoulder. "But now," he went on, turning to the priest who had been taking notes, "before we eat, write down a letter." Closing his eyes, he began slowly enough so that the quill of the priest could keep pace with him:

"MAGNUS, BY THE GRACE OF GOD, KING OF NORWAY, SWEDEN AND SKAANE, *sends to all men who see or hear this letter, good health and happiness.*

"*We desire to make known to you that you,* PAUL KNUTSON, *are to take the men who shall go in the royal trading ship, whether they be named or not named, from my bodyguard and also from among the retainers of other men whom you may wish to take on the voyage, and that* PAUL KNUTSON, *who shall be the* COMMANDANT *upon the ship, shall have full authority to select the men whom he finds best suited to accompany him, whether as officers or men.*"

"You see, Paul," he said, breaking off, "I am giving you full authority to take whomever you like, but I hope you will take some of my bodyguard to go in my place. Would to God I, myself, might be at your side!" Magnus sighed and continued, "Let's see, where was I?"

The priest lifted his head.

"—officers or men," he repeated.

"Yes, well, to continue:

"*We ask that you will accept this,* OUR COMMAND, *with a right good will for the cause, inasmuch as we do it for the honor of* GOD *and for the sake of our soul and for the sake of our predecessors who, in Greenland, established Christianity and have maintained it to this time, and we will not now let it perish in our days. Know this for truth, that whoever defies this,* OUR COMMAND, *shall meet with our serious displeasure and thereupon receive full punishment.*"

He turned to the regent, Orm Ostenson, an older man who had spoken little.

"Is there anything which I should have added?"

"No, my lord. That gives Paul Knutson full authority in everything."

"Then read over the letter and seal it with the royal seal, and give it to Paul. Paul, show that to the merchants when you are taking on your cargo. My treasury will honor whatever you need, both as to cargo and for your expedition. Of course, if you return, you will bring an exchange. Walrus tusks and narwhal horns are always in demand, ermine, foxskins, walrus hides, and I should be glad if you could include a live polar bear, the younger, the better—two cubs, say."

"I doubt if that would make up a full cargo for the ship, sir," said the regent. "Probably you will have to take on a certain amount of butter, and sheepskins and hides to ballast the vessel."

Paul shrugged his shoulders.

"I am not a merchant," he said impatiently. "You have a royal agent, I believe, at the settlement. He will attend to the bartering and the cargo for Bergen, not I, though I shall remember the white cubs. What interests me are not logs of wood and barrels of wine, but men, the forty men who are to go with me to follow the western colonists!"

Paul looked about him, and his face had changed; it was hard and assured, as positive as a sword. Even his voice had in it the confidence of the leader. This was Paul Knutson as his own followers knew him, resourceful, sagacious, and filled with savage joy in the face of battle. Norwegians and Swedes, the king's men, shouted their answer:

"Take me!" "Take me! Our fathers fought side by side!" "No, me! Paul Knutson! I have served you before!" "Me, Paul, of the king's guard!" The shouts struck against one another like the din of swords against shields, until Paul, laughing, held up both hands for silence.

"Where all are eager to go, I must do the choosing. First, to represent the king, I take Orm Karlsson and hope that he may be as willing to follow as I to lead."

The glance of the two men met and locked like horns. Orm Karlsson had broad lands and a new-married wife. If he regretted now having taunted Paul, if he hesitated one instant for Magnus to say that he could not be spared, the hesitation did not appear in face or voice.

"Willingly, and God prosper our undertaking!" he answered loudly.

"Benedikt Karlsson!"

This was too much. There were but the two brothers. Orm turned to the king.

"If I go, Magnus, Benedikt must stay at home to look after our affairs."

Magnus nodded, but Benedikt, the unpredictable, laughed.

"You stay, then, Orm. For I am going."

"You will stain your brocaded robes!" snorted the elder Karlsson, but he said nothing more, for now Nicolas Byrgeson's thin voice was heard.

"I wish to go, Paul."

Paul looked down at him with kindly contempt.

"This journey is beyond you, Nicolas, I fear."

But the man persisted.

"It is the will of God. When I first saw and heard the Greenlanders, I knew that I had been summoned to

serve Christ in far-off places. I have had such dreams!
No, Paul Knutson, my sword arm may be weak, but
you know the old adage,

> *" 'Courage is better*
> *Than the power of sword*
> *Where the angry must fight;*
> *For I saw a bold man win*
> *Victory, with a blunt sword.'*

I am your blunt sword, Paul; you cannot leave me
behind."

The Norwegian laughed and clapped Nicolas on his
thin shoulder.

"Come then, friend, since I cannot leave you behind.
But be warned now, we cannot stop for any man's
weakness. The ailing must be left by the way, you
understand."

"I understand," said the Swede with an exalted look.

Magnus said in the same tone, "God will give him
the necessary strength."

"I hope so, indeed," Paul agreed briskly. "Now for
the rest. Vinalde Algotsson, are you not near neighbor
to Orm Karlsson? Very well, man, I know you for a
cheerful campaigner, and let us take Johan Markusson
so that he may smell coming trouble in the wind for us.
Here are five Swedes to represent the king; Orm, bring
seven more with you as you may see fit—lesser men.
There must be good milk as well as cream in the bowl.
Now for Norwegians, for, as you said, Magnus, this is
first and last a Norwegian affair."

"Will you not take my priest, Sira Audun, a young
man, strong and very devout?" the king pleaded,
quickly.

But Paul shook his head.

"No, no, my lord. None goes with me but my own fat, fearless Sira Andres. I have seen him fight a bear with a trencher knife, once upon a time. I have chosen Swedes from among your attendants at your request; for the rest, I wish the men I know and have fought with—men of my own neighborhood, and their sons, not men who have gone to court, but those who have fought the Russians with me from the same deck."

"Then you must take me, Paul Knutson," said a voice, a strange voice, almost like a sleepwalker's, unreal to the ear.

All eyes turned and there stood the page, Olav Sigurdson, staring at Paul with his black unseeing stare.

Paul started and raised his hand as though to cross himself, but refrained. If a dead man had spoken, he could not have been taken more by surprise.

"No, Olav," he said almost gently. "No, you are too young."

"Too young?" the other repeated. "No, I am not too young. My father, Sigurd Olavson, had fought the Lapps and the Russian pirates at my age. My father," he repeated slowly, with a curious threatening sound in his voice, "my father, Sigurd, your friend, called 'Sigurd the Bold.'"

Paul drew his hand across his forehead. He was sweating. Then he said sternly, "Sigurd, as all men know, was my friend until he betrayed me and Norway, and proved himself a coward in the fight in the Narrow Straits."

"He was never a coward! And had you not been a false friend, Paul Knutson, you would have killed the man who called him one. But you were the first to dishonor him when he was dead. He did not order his ship out of that close-fought fight in order to escape,

but so that he might circle the island and come upon
the enemy in the rear!"

"And for that, there is no word but Eirik's whom we
picked up on a rock after Sigurd's ship had been pursued
by the Russians and sunk. And who would believe
Eirik, the Lapp? No, no, Olav, heavy was my heart on
the day I knew I had been betrayed by my own friend.
But I, myself, saw his ship go by, and shouted to him
to come back, and, above the battle din, heard him still
urge on the rowers. No, a coward at the last was Sigurd,
and I want no more dealings with his blood."

Still came the boy's haunted voice, "Your word
against Eirik's, and I say you lie and Eirik speaks the
truth. Let God judge between us. I undertake the ordeal,
an ordeal of ice and cold, instead of the ordeal of fire.
If I return alive and have never turned from danger,
you will acknowledge that my father was a wronged man
and no coward. If I die, God has judged my father and
me, and you are upheld."

"No! No!" shouted Paul Knutson. "I do not wish
you aboard the Knarr. I wish to forget you both and
the sorrow of that betrayal. Get out of my sight, and
let me hear no more of you."

Magnus said calmly, "I am sorry, Paul, but it no
longer rests with you. The boy has appealed to God.
He must have a chance to prove his father's innocence."

Paul swung on the king.

"You would take a Lapp no-man's word before
mine?"

Magnus smiled.

"It is not a question of whose word I take, but whom
God will justify, he who looks into the hearts of men. In
his sight, Eirik may be as important as you or I, my
Paul."

"You take a great responsibility, my lord. This expedition to serve God grows leaky with court dandies and the sons of cowards. Will this whelp not betray me as did his father? He hates me now. In your presence, he has called me a liar and a false friend. He will stick a knife between my ribs some dark night."

Magnus did not answer, but beckoned to the boy.

"Will you swear dutiful service, Olav?" he asked gravely.

"To you, my lord, but not to him."

The boy knelt down and put his hands between the king's.

"In the name of God, I swear to serve Paul Knutson in all things, and to forward this expedition to bring back the lost Greenlanders to the worship of our faith. If I return, having never shown fear, Paul Knutson is to acknowledge his mistake, and the name of my father, Sigurd Olavson, is to be cleared of all shame and blame in the sight of men. Let God hear my words."

The boy rose, and the king took his right hand and stretched out his left toward Paul, who made a wry face, but placed his right hand in the king's, who joined it with the boy's. The two hands held together for a moment. Both were ice-cold. Then they dropped apart.

"So be it," said Paul. "A man never knows when he wakes in the morning what a day may bring. With my lord's permission, I will return to my lodgings now, and this afternoon, go down to the Knarr to start preparations. We should be able to put to sea by the middle of May."

"Go, of course," said Magnus. "I am sorry you are displeased, but I see no way to refuse the boy when he has taken his father's case to the court of heaven. On the whole, however, a great deal of ground has been

cleared this morning. With you, my Paul, at the head
of the expedition, much worry is already taken off my
mind. Real happiness fills me to think that once again
the Devil is to be robbed."

"That remains to be seen, Magnus," Paul replied,
bowing, "but I am grateful for your confidence. Until
tomorrow, then. I will report in the morning in what
condition I find the ship."

He turned, catching his wife's gentle glance among
the coiffed matrons standing to one side. She, in turn,
made her adieus to the queen and then, taking her
daughter's hand, moved out from among the clustered
ladies to join her husband. Ingrid Ivasdatter was a
slender, rather frail woman with a face nearly as white
as the linen that covered her head, but the young Ingrid
was tall and ruddy like her father. Only the hair that
hung smooth and heavy about her shoulders and down
to her girdle was honey-colored like her mother's. She
was so young that she was still long-legged like a colt,
and her face had a little of the child's roundness left in
the cheeks. But her eyes were not a child's. There always
seemed a smile in them, though her mouth was grave,
and they were smiling now as she followed her mother
into the open hall. Once free of the ladies, she pulled
her fingers from her mother's light grasp.

"I have someone to speak to for a moment," she
murmured, turning back toward the men.

"Ingrid!" exclaimed her father, reaching out an affec-
tionate hand to detain her, but she slipped by him, her
eyes smiling into his. She had on a red gown and a green
cloak embroidered all about the border, and held at the
neck with a clasp of garnets; her undersleeves were also
of green, but of a very light shade, like young willow
leaves.

Swiftly she walked to where Olav was standing, once more a little apart, and pulled his sleeve.

"Olav," she said when he paid no attention, "Olav."

He swung to face her, and his face changed as though he had found himself looking into the sun on Easter Day.

"Ingrid!" he exclaimed, and then said nothing more.

Her eyes did not lose their smiling look.

"Olav, I wanted you to know that I do not hold our betrothal to be broken. When you return, I shall marry you as our fathers long ago arranged when we were little children."

Her father and mother had, by this time, joined them, and Paul said, angrily, "What maiden nonsense is this, Ingrid? You will marry whom I say, like an obedient daughter."

"Only for Olav will I wear the bridal wreath. If you wish me to go to the nuns, I will obey you willingly, but I will marry no man but Olav Sigurdson, as God sees me."

And taking a bracelet from her wrist, she gave it to Olav before her father pulled her away.

Chapter 3

Hestnaes

Olav lay in his bed at Hestnaes, awake and weary in the dawn. He heard the cocks crowing from the farmyard, and after all these months at court, he could still recognize the triumphant peal of the old cock, and the more broken answer of the one they called Fireback. But there were voices new to him. They made a chorus of high shoutings, a clamor of delight, sometimes four or five birds crowing at almost the same instant. What pleasure he had once felt in that sound!

He lay very still, the fingers of his right hand just touching Ingrid's bracelet, which he wore on his left forearm. It was of silver and wound twice around his arm, ending in lions' heads. The smith who had made it was a master workman; the heads were fierce and small, their silver faces were decorated with manes and eyes of gold, and in their open mouths could be seen small, curling gold tongues. Now he could see nothing of them in the darkness of his bed behind the embroidered curtains, but he could feel the small heads with the tips of his fingers. They reassured him after the nightmares from which he had wakened.

In the bed across from him, he could hear his mother saying her morning prayers, repeating the Latin words with the French accent which made her seem something of a stranger, even to him, her son. Ingeborg, her woman, was already moving about the room beyond the beds. He could hear her sniffling in the morning chill and raking over the ashes in the long hearth in the middle of the floor, finding the last embers hidden away, and strengthening them with shreds of birch bark for the morning fire.

He would not move yet. He lay like a statue, straight out in his bed, his hands on his breast, the fingers touching Ingrid's gift. He ached from yesterday's long ride through the mud. The whole countryside had seemed like a huge sponge under the tender May-day sky, but the thickets were showing small green leaves, just opening from their tight buds and transparent to the light; there were long tassels on the birch trees, and everywhere the new grass rose, green and beautiful through the matted old grass of last year.

But Sokka's hoofs slipped and squelched in endless mud. Olav rode with a tightened rein to keep the mare from falling, and he was splashed with mud even across the face. It was long since he had been all day in the saddle, and he was stiff and sore when at last he dismounted at Hestnaes, with Eirik holding Sokka's bridle and grinning up at him in the light of the wide-open door.

Yet he had ridden that day in a mood more cheerful than had been usual with him since his father's death. He was aware again of the country about him, of the dark steep fells overhead and the snow which still lay in the shadow of the heights; he saw the swollen streams and heard their loud laughter. He looked into the faces of those few travelers whom he met, and returned their greetings. He watched the smoke rise from the farmsteads he passed, standing back among their clusters of bakehouses and storehouses, cookhouses, spinning houses, barns and sheepfolds. Since he had put his hands between the hands of Magnus in the king's house, and had been accepted for the Greenland voyage, he had, in part at least, returned to the world about him. Now there was something in which he might serve his father.

Then why had the old nightmares returned? Always he was trying to get somewhere, and he could not. Something held him back. He strained forward. His heart seemed ready to burst, but still he seemed to be losing ground. Then the salt wave rose over him and he was borne down and down; even in the depths of the sea he tried to move toward his goal, but the Margygi, smiling through their floating hair, held him back with webbed hands, and the monstrous octopuses wrapped him about with their tentacles.

Olav woke up at last, panting and shaken. The old dream, the old dream! The spirit of Sigurd Olavson entered into his son and travailed still. So had Sigurd felt on that day in the Narrow Straits when his strategy had failed, and he had tried without success to regain the battle where his friends seemed doomed to defeat. So, drowning, had he still struggled to go on, even among the horrors of the underseas.

Olav was exhausted by the visitation. Unburied, dishonored, where lay his father's bones? He crossed himself and knelt, saying his morning prayer, but so low that he hoped no one would hear him. Yet his mother must have been listening for him to wake, for with the last amen she drew the curtains and greeted him lovingly.

The hearth room was gray in the morning light which came only from the venthole in the gable over the fire in the center of the floor. His mother had always wanted a new hall with a built-in fireplace in the wall such as there was in the king's house, and windows with glass and a great guest chamber above. Sigurd had promised to build one where the spinning house now stood, but the trouble with Russia had put off the building, and now it would never be done.

Olav liked the old hearth house well enough. The women had already taken the board down from the wall and placed it on the trestles, and were bringing in the porridge and milk, ale and bread. They all came to speak with him and to welcome him home; the men, too, came up to him, bringing with them the smell of the byre.

"Today they are planning to bring the cattle out of the barns," his mother told him. "The grass is strong enough, Eirik says."

Olav smiled at his mother.

"You speak like a good Norwegian," he said. Poor Helga Petersdatter, as they called her! She had been one of the queen's ladies brought with her from France,

and when Sigurd Olavson courted her, she had not
guessed that the handsome young man with velvet cap
under his arm was only one of the men she was marrying.
There were at least two others; one, the farmer at Hestnaes, who spoke of plowing and planting, pig-killing
and ale-brewing with his men, as her father in France
had never done; the other was the Sigurd whose warship
lay in a sheltered bight, and who went out with his
friend and neighbor, Paul Knutson, for weeks at a time
on watch for the ships of the pirates, whether Lapp or
Finn or Russian, which sometimes stole along the coast
in the fog and robbed the farms by the shore, killing
the men and often enough carrying away the women.

Her father, heaven knows, had known fighting and
had ridden often in the jousts, but she had never seen
him show this fierce delight in armor and battle which
these men felt.

But through all the new life, when the kitchen girls
called her Helga Petersdatter—no one, not even Sigurd,
could say Helöise—through the dark endless winters
and the smells of the farmyard and the bright summers,
she had remained arch and gay and gentle as Sigurd
had first known her. But without him she had withered,
and there was a bitterness mixed with the sweetness of
her voice; she talked much of France and of the orchards
in flower about her father's castle, and spoke sharply
to the women in the weaving house when they whispered and dawdled.

She frowned now when Eirik slipped into the room
late and took his place on the bench opposite the high
seats where she sat with Olav, but the man greeted her
with sly composure.

"A good day for the cattle, mistress," he said, breaking off a great hunk of black bread from the loaf. "A

single crow is strutting about in the barnyard and that is a good sign."

Helga Petersdatter nodded without speaking, but Olav said, "I am glad that the poor beasts are getting out of the barn early this year."

Eirik cocked his head and regarded him. He was a short man with a broad dark face, narrow, slanted black eyes and a sparse beard. No one knew how old he was nor where he came from, but people said—not to his face—that he was a Lapp and a wizard, and that nothing could kill him. Sigurd Olavson had brought him back from one of his forays long ago, and since then he had served at Hestnaes, or perhaps ruled. Sigurd would listen to him when he would take the advice of no other man, and it was he who had lived to be taken off the rocky isle by Paul Knutson after his master's ship had gone down.

Now he grinned at Olav. "I shall go with you," he said.

Olav's eyes opened wide. Last evening he had not spoken of the expedition to anyone, and news did not travel from Bergen, so far in so short a time.

His mother turned to him. "You are going away, my son?"

He had meant to speak of it a little later, but now he told her of what had happened at the king's house and explained that he had returned home to ask her blessing, and to gather the necessary supplies for the voyage.

"You will be away for some months?"

"Perhaps for some years," he answered soberly.

She put her hands over her heart.

"What shall I do? With Sigurd gone, and now with you leaving me? On every side, the neighbors press me

in since your father's disgrace. It has become a virtue
in them to claim one of our fields here or a mountain
meadow there."

Eirik again spoke up, "You need not worry, Helga
Petersdatter. Since Olav has called upon the judgment
of God, his lands will be safe enough until he returns."

Now how had Eirik known about the judgment of
God? For, in telling the story, Olav said only that he
was to be one of the expedition. But now his mother
turned to him, her face burning with joy.

"You will justify your father? Oh, Olav, my lamb, go
then, go! And my blessing and prayers will follow you!"
And she covered her face with her hands and wept.

But soon she dried her eyes, and took him with her
into the loft of the granary. There they opened two
chests and took out the rolls of heavy cloth which she
and her women had woven, and they chose what he
would take. She brought a cloak lined with wolf skin,
very heavy and warm, a scarlet hood lined with wolf
skin also, which had been Sigurd's, and lastly chose
from a pile of hides the leather for his boots.

Then opening another chest, Helga brought out a
sword with a fine hilt and scabbard.

"My father's," she said. "Take it with you."

Olav drew the blade from the sheath but before he
could speak, a voice behind them said, "It is not strong
enough for a Norseman."

Neither was startled. At Hestnaes, Eirik might be
expected to speak out of any shadow. And as usual,
what Eirik said was true; in the end, a sword was found
in the chest which had belonged to Olav's grandfather,
who was also an Olav. There were words engraved along
the blade and the boy, who had been taught by the
parish priest, Sira Björgulf, leaned over them in the

cob-webbed light, and read, "Draw me in the service of Christ."

"Ah!" Olav drew in his breath sharply, staring at the sword. "This is the one for me."

Eirik looked at him from small, sardonic eyes.

"You care far more for your father's name, my Olav, than for this crusade of the king's."

Olav did not answer at once, but stood, still staring down at the blade. Then he looked up quietly.

"The two tasks are one, Eirik."

The man slapped his thigh.

"Mistress, you should have made a priest of your son. He has a priest's tongue." Yet Eirik grinned to himself, not dissatisfied.

"Let me put on your sword belt," said Helga, and she knelt on the dusty floor, fastening the heavy silver buckles, while Olav stood looking off into the distance, feeling for the first time the companionship of his own sword against his thigh. His father had trained him well with spear and battle-ax, bow and sword. But before this, he had had no sword of his own, only a long dagger with a silver-gilt handle.

When she was done, Olav lifted his mother to her feet and kissed her hands in the court manner which the French courtiers used, and she kissed him upon either cheek.

"You will make a fine knight, my son," she said wistfully, "and bring back your father's honor from Greenland."

"If Olav proves a good fighter, the knight part may go hang from a willow tree," Eirik joined in, impudently, for like most Norsemen, he had little patience with the French words and practices which spread like a light haze outward from the court.

Helga made no answer, but motioning to the man to bring the rolls of wool and the hide with him, she opened the door again and went out onto the balcony where she stood with Olav for a moment before descending into the courtyard.

How springlike the air was! A hawk passed overhead against a cloud, uttering a thin, small, complaining cry, and the high fells seemed so near that they leaned over the roofs. From the barnyard beyond there was a clamor of voices, advice shouted, and calls of encouragement and sometimes laughter.

"They are all idle," she said. "As soon as my back is turned, everyone slips out on any excuse."

"But the cattle are being brought out," said Olav eagerly. "Come, Mother, and watch. It means that winter is over."

She shook her head, having no liking for putting foot in the barnyard. "You go," she said. "I wish to begin cutting out your clothes so that we may commence work at once. If you see Groa or Aashield, tell them to come to the weaving house. Immediately!"

All the men and women of Hestnaes were grouped in a big half-moon before the door of the barn—the women behind the men, pretending to be frightened as the young black bull was led out. The poor creature was so thin that it was all he could do to keep to his feet. He staggered and would have fallen if the herdsmen had not held him up, one on either side. When at last he had staggered as far as the pasture, he stood with his legs far apart, holding himself up, and then stretched out his neck and gave a weak bellow, at which the people applauded. Then he reached down and, in a fumbling, uncertain way, pulled at the new grass.

One cow followed him on her feet, but the rest had

to be carried out on a hurdle one by one, amid great haulings and pushings, and proddings, and grunts and sweat from the young men who brought them out, and pushed them finally onto the grass where, for the most part, they lay eating what was within reach of their soft muzzles.

Dirty from the long winter in their stalls, cavernous, pathetic, the herd of Hestnaes breathed in the May air, felt the sun once more on their sunken sides, and tasted again fresh food after the long scarcity of winter. It was so everywhere. The hay that could be brought in was never at all sufficient. When their strength had returned, they would go up to the farm meadows in the high hills, and there they would become fat and sleek again, while the lonely dairy house filled its casks one by one with sour milk and curds, and the shelves grew heavy with cheeses.

Olav was glad that he had not gone before the cows were out. Their return to pasture seemed a good omen for his venture, and today there would be no more low moaning from the darkness of the barn. The sheep were already in their fields and looked at him with agate eyes when he came to the gate. What was the old saying? "A sheepless household starves." Well, Hestnaes had many sheep. This was his land and these were his creatures. Would he live to see them again?

The week that Olav spent at Hestnaes went more quickly than he could have wished. His mother and her women were busy most of the day in the weaving house, making clothes for his departure, and in the evenings, Helga embroidered bands and cuffs with designs of rearing horses and hounds, "For you must not appear among the others dressed as a poor man's son," she said, looking at him with pride.

She seemed to have no misgivings, but Olav did not share her confidence. He had never been farther from his home than Bergen and now no man could say how far they were going, or if they would ever return from this voyage. And he wondered if he could indeed vindicate his father, or might he not show himself a coward, and so disgrace Hestnaes irretrievably and forever? The dream of his father returned almost nightly, but now the struggle seemed to take place on a frozen sea, and cold was part of the horror.

Word came that farther down the valley, Paul Knutson was having some difficulty in assembling the necessary number of men. Despite the king's authorization, people had little stomach for the Greenland voyage, and less still for what lay beyond. Paul had gone so far as to enroll outlaws—at least it was said that a young man named Ulf Kyrning was going. He was a hot-head who had killed a man in a fight last winter, and had been sentenced at the *thing* to three-years' exile from Norway. So Ulf was going, and who knew what others outside the law? Olav, seeing Paul Knutson after church—his wife and young Ingrid had been left at Bergen—went up to him and asked permission to take Eirik with him.

"That Lapp?" Paul demanded.

"We may have need of his runes where we are going," Olav replied boldly.

Paul laughed. "They say that water cannot drown him nor steel cut him. Well, bring him along, Olav. Though to tell you the truth, I cannot look at his broad face without remembering things I had rather forget."

"He is a good man," said Olav. "My father always declared that he could row for three days without food or drink."

When Olav spoke with Paul Knutson, the moody
dream that held him nowadays was broken, and he
stood straight and his dark eyes stared into Paul's eyes
from under a frowning brow. In his challenging look,
there was none of the respect of a boy for an older man,
nor of a follower for his leader. His glance was the
fighter's glance measuring an adversary just before the
first sword stroke, and in return Paul gave him a forbidding and icy stare from his blue eyes. Now he
turned away without any parting word, but Olav was
well satisfied.

If Olav was content to have Eirik go with him, it was
more than was Helga Petersdatter. When she saw, on
the morning of departure, another horse behind Sokka
and Eirik dressed for travel, she turned white as her
coif.

"What is this, Olav?" she demanded in her broken
speech which had never lost its French cast. "You are
surely not taking with you that bird of ill omen?"

She spoke loudly, not caring that Eirik heard.

Olav laid a silencing hand on her arm.

"Hush, Mother. Be still. Eirik has served us well."

But his mother would not be still.

"Well?" she repeated with growing wildness. "When
he returned to Hestnaes without a scratch, while your
father and all the rest died? I had not so much as Sigurd
Olavson's dead body to put in his empty grave in the
churchyard. But this time, if the wizard returns home
alone, I shall discover for myself if it is true that he
cannot die!"

Eirik made her a low bow.

"You need not trouble yourself, mistress. Have an
empty grave for me dug at the foot of Sigurd's empty
grave. I shall not return."

Chapter 4

Landfall

"Who are the maidens
That walk over the reefs,
And journey along the fiords?
These white-hooded women
Have a hard bed,
And make little stir in calm weather."

THE OLD riddling rime ran through Olav's head as
he stood at the rail of the Knarr, looking back
along the coast where the waves were running
in orderly rows, like coifed women on their way to
church. It was warm, and he was glad to stand in the

shadow of the striped sail with its golden weather vane cock at the top of the mast. Everything was gay with a late spring exuberance, and the sea gulls which followed, crying in their wake, seemed whiter than curds in the May sunlight. With his right hand, he touched Ingrid's bracelet. When the ship set sail he had seen her, but only from a distance. Her mother had held her back from coming to him, but she had waved him goodby, looking very grown-up, and smiling at him with the particularly desperate smile natural to women at parting.

Olav had never been at sea before, yet it seemed to him now as though he must have been born at sea, with a ship for his first cradle, so natural and good did the life seem to him. He never wearied of waves, nor of winds as they sailed straight into the west. From first to last, they had a lucky voyage. They saw Shetland far to the south, the mountains of the Faroes to the north; then for a while they saw no landmark, but at last there were gulls again and a whale or two spouting, and they knew that they were passing Iceland, out of sight in the fog.

West, west, west. Day followed day, and once they rode out a storm. At its worst, Eirik cut a rune upon a stick and, wetting it with blood from his left arm, threw it overboard, and the wind began to moderate almost immediately. He said that he had seen a witch riding a whale among the waves and that she was the cause of the storm. His stick had wounded her mount, making it sound, and the witch had been drowned. So ran Eirik's tale, but it was not much heeded. Sira Andres at the bow had been praying, while Eirik worked his magic at the stern, and most of the company attributed the calmer weather to the priest's prayers. Benedikt

Karlsson even went so far as to say that the wind was hauling into another quarter at the time, and that every storm blew itself out, sooner or later.

The storm had forced them off their course, but Paul judged not too far, and with good hope they again headed the high, carved dragon's head of the prow westward. Among the common men, Olav was treated courteously, though with a little reservation. Son of a dishonored man, squired by a Lapp wizard, he stood apart from the rest, and the men of substance tended to consider him as a useless boy who had forced himself upon them. Only the courtier, Benedikt Karlsson among the Swedes, would stop now and then to exchange unnecessary words with him; and Ulf Kyrning treated him with easy comradeship, being himself out of fortune, although one would never have guessed it from his carefree, noisy speech.

It was this Ulf who first sighted a snow-capped mountain which was lost again in fog. Paul turned southward, keeping well out from the drifting ice pack and bidding Sira Andres pray that no east wind should come up to wreck them upon that shore, where so many men had died. Two days later they saw the massive, white-topped block of the Hvarf mountains, and rounded the Cape, past Point Herjolfsnes and into the harbor of Sand. Its little church—standing near the water—was built of stone, in a style that seemed strange to Olav, who was used to wooden churches.

The farmer of Herjolfsnes, and all the older men of the countryside were there to meet them, as were the women and children, the dogs, and even an overcurious goat or two, drawn by the excitement.

Ulf said in Olav's ear, "By heaven, we are come into a land of trolls!"

And indeed the people were very small, coming only to the shoulders of the newcomers, and seeming smaller than ever against the wide landscape of green fields and uprearing mountains and the blue sea, scattered with bare rocky islets, like the backs of basking sea creatures, beyond which drifted other islets of floe ice.

Olav was glad to be ashore again, to feel turf under his feet, and to exchange greetings with these small smiling people, half beside themselves with joy at seeing once more the royal ship.

"No vessel has come here for years," the headman told them in his barbarous speech. "We were growing afraid that you Norwegians had forgotten us! No! No! I know you would not do that! When we saw your sail, I had sheep killed, and we have seals' flesh and reindeer if you prefer. The younger men are off to the Northern Hunting Grounds for the summer hunt of narwhals and walrus, but we still hunt a little here. Come with me to Herjolfnes farm, up there against the mountain, and we shall make what cheer we can. But there's no ale, only crowberry wine, if you can put up with that," and he made a face at which Paul laughed, quickly reassuring his host.

"You furnish meat, my friend, and we shall furnish drink," he said, and turned aside to order ashore a couple of hogsheads of ale.

Paul rode on one of the shaggy little horses and so did Nicolas Byrgeson, looking ill and worn from the voyage, for the life on board ship did not agree with the queasy stomach of the king's counselor. The rest walked, and Olav was surprised to see how green the grass grew and how fat were the cattle and sheep. There were no trees anywhere, only scrub willows and birch, but Olav was delighted with the broad, bright landscape. The farmhouse was a fine one, built of stone, with separate rooms, and the walls of the chamber where they sat were paneled in wood, and ornamented by an embroidered hanging which showed the waves overwhelming Pharaoh's host. Fresh meat seemed delicious after the food aboard ship. Olav was glad to be among strangers where his story was not yet known and his garments and bearing made him appear to be a person of some importance.

But next morning they left for the Eastern Settlement, sailing along the coast, filled with wonder at its wild magnificence, until they came to Einarsfjord. They continued up the fiord, past high mountains and scattered farms, at last arriving at Gardar, where stood the Cathedral of St. Nicholas, with the episcopal residence at right angles to it.

Again a small excited crowd, lacking most of the younger men, met them, this time headed by the priest, Ivar Bardson, steward of the bishopric, in full charge since the death of old Bishop Arne. He was a Norwegian; a thick, vigorous man who seemed more man of action than scholar. With him came Thorvald Jonsson, chief yeoman at the great farm of Brattahlid in the next fiord, a Greenlander descended from one of the men who had first come out from Iceland with Eirik the Red, and now living at Eirik's homestead, the richest in Greenland.

After everyone had gone into the church to give thanks for the safe voyage, Ivar led them to the bishop's house and there again a great feast had been spread in the hall. People had arrived on horseback and on foot over the narrow roads, and by vessel from farms on the islands and along the fiords.

"News! News!" exclaimed Ivar. "We are devouring

you already with our eyes. So—we see what fashions men wear now in Norway."

"And our women have sent dresses to your women," Paul said, smiling down the table from the high seat where he sat beside the priest.

"But tell us if the king will do anything about the Western Settlement," demanded Thorvald, "or is he only interested in taking tax goods from us?"

"The Western Settlement can wait!" Ivar shouted. "First I must hear of Norway and of the bishop, and of the war which the king meant to make on Russia."

"That was over years ago," Paul said. "We were victorious and christened many to our faith, but then we left for home too early and our victory melted from us. Magnus planned a new war and the Pope blessed the undertaking, but the people will not go because of the plague." He told them of the affairs of the kingdom, while everyone listened breathlessly, whether the news was of last winter or of seven years ago. Then people began to shout out questions as to relatives and whether they were alive or dead, but Thorvald broke in again, impatiently.

"And now as to *our* affairs! Did our ship reach Bergen? It has not returned, but they planned to spend this winter in Iceland."

So the talk swung to Greenland, and Paul told of how Magnus Eirikson had grieved when he saw the hammer of Thor upon the soapstone bowl, and had sworn to bring the lost colony back to their faith.

"I thought that would fetch him!" Thorvald exclaimed. He had been drinking horn after horn of ale and was ready for boasting. "I myself sent the bowl and told them what to say. Though, mind you, it came not from the Western Settlement, but from my own house at Brattahlid."

"What's this?" Paul asked sharply, turning to Ivar Bardson. "Is it not true that the people at the Western Settlement had returned to unlawful practices?"

The priest sat for a while in silence, the tips of his fingers just touching. Then he spoke.

"You in Norway do not quite understand how it is here. The people are good Christians, yes, even in the Western Settlement. I am sure that they were, in the main, good Christians still. But the country is so vast— so cold. We do not know what lies beyond us in any direction! Even after three hundred and more years, we are only about three thousand souls scattered between the ice-cold sea and the ice cap that pushes almost to the shore. When you hear the roar of an iceberg, calved by a glacier in some fiord, it is not a good Christian sound. And then come the long winters when the sun lies far off in a little ring to the south! One feels that perhaps Christ did not have Greenland in mind when he preached in the Holy Land. Here among the fogs and the ice, the old gods seem always near. I did not understand it myself when I first came here, but now I understand."

He paused again, and at last said into the silence, "If a woman says an old charm at her buttermaking, or a man carves a hammer on his work, it does not mean that they are not good Christians."

Nicolas Byrgeson said loudly, "I am ashamed to hear such words from the mouth of a priest!"

Thorvald laughed and drank more ale.

"Wait until you have been alone for a few days and nights on a floating ice cake, my friend!" he said, and drank again. He wiped the foam from his mouth and went on, "Alone, with your little boat caved in, and nothing to be seen, perhaps, but some great white bear pulling himself up onto the ice from the black water."

"It is true," said Ivar Bardson. "No priest should say such things. But perhaps no priest should live here so far from the world."

"Wherever the Sacrament is taken, there is God!" said Nicolas, in the same high rebuking voice; but the priest turned on him.

"For two years now, we have had no wine and no bread. You do not yet realize, Swede, that you are at the ends of the world."

Nicolas gaped at him like a fish newly drawn from the water, Olav thought. From a seat beside Thorvald, he had been listening eagerly. The king's counselor had never imagined such things, and now he said in a lower voice, "We have brought much wine and grain with us."

"They will be most welcome so long as they last," said the other, sadly. "And in return, I hope that you will never feel the Older Things leaning at your shoulder."

Paul broke into the conversation, questioning again as to what they had found at the Western Settlement. The story that the priest told was much the same as the men had told at court. In the middle of the account, Thorvald whistled to an unusually long-legged, rough, gray-coated hound, which came out from under the table.

"There is the dog which met us at the beach. We call him Smyrill, the Sparrow Hawk. He is the last of the Western Settlement breed. If you go, you shall take him with you. He might be useful in tracing the people."

Someone threw a bone toward Smyrill, but he made no attempt to catch it. He was staring at Thorvald. "What do you want with me?" his eyes seemed to be asking. "Where, among all these people, is my master? Why have you brought me here?"

Olav saw the lost look in the dog's eyes, that bewildered brooding look of a creature from whom its assurances have been taken, suddenly and all at once.

He reached out and put his hand on the narrow head. Whatever else might be small here, it was not this dog. Smyrill stood higher than any hound Olav had ever seen. Now the hound turned his head to look at the boy. Quietly their eyes met in a long stare. Then, with a sigh, the great beast took two steps and lay down at Olav's feet.

Chapter 5

Eirik in Danger

OLAV always avoided speaking to Paul Knutson when he could, and never stood near him if it could be avoided, but on this day he sought him out by the water front at Gardar and asked for permission to go hunting with Thorvald, the master of Brattahlid, next to whom he had sat at dinner the night before.

Paul pulled his lip. "I suppose you may. But be back tomorrow. I plan to sail the next morning and will wait for no one."

Olav nodded. "I understand. And Eirik?"

"Where the horse goes, the horse's tail will follow,"

Paul said, and then, as if feeling that he had been too good-humored, he added, "there is no need to tell you to keep out of trouble."

A quick flush came to Olav's face, and he stared at Paul in that blind way the man had first noticed at the king's house.

It was Paul who turned away. He had much to do, for the Knarr was being unloaded. Nicolas Byrgeson stood on the dock, bleating to everyone to be careful of his precious stained-glass window. The women were at him to find the chest with the robes of which he had spoken. The men seemed to think most of steel and ale. Their knives wore down against the whetstone and could not be replaced. Now they stood along the shore, watchful as a flock of gulls when the fishermen are gutting their catch. Everything brought out of the hold was of greatest interest, yet, being men and not gulls, they held back, not wishing to appear greedy, waiting to see what the ship had brought and how it would be apportioned; and meanwhile, reckoning inwardly, what weight of walrus and narwhal tusks, and how many white bearskins they had in their storehouses to offer in return.

The great plain of Gardar between the fiords had not seen so many people for years. The strangers filled the bishop's house, but relatives and friends crowded the four farms, or slept in their boats or in temporary shelters rigged up along the shore. It was like a fair day at home.

"And I suppose I am the dancing bear," thought Paul, good-humoredly, knowing that so many eyes followed his slightest motion, and so many ears listened for his every word.

But Olav and Eirik turned their backs on the unload-

ing and followed the short broad figure of Thorvald
Jonsson across the plain, to his boat in Eiriksfjord.
Olav and the Greenlander had struck up an acquaint-
ance at the bishop's table the evening before, and ex-
pansive with ale, Thorvald had invited the boy to go
for a hunt with him in the high valleys. He had left the
arrangements for bartering with a younger brother who
had a gift for such things.

"Sverre is a trader and will do better than I. Besides,
since I said that the bowl was from Brattahlid, I notice
that many of you look askance at me, especially that
old sheep in the fine red gown and green shoes."

"Looking down his nose is Nicolas' way," said Olav
with a laugh. He was glad to get clear of the others for
a while. After a long voyage where one rubbed against
another person at every turn, it was good to walk
freely in such an empty country. He liked to have
Smyrill at his heels, to raise his eyes to a hawk's flight
outlined against the snow of the mountains, to feel
Eirik beside him like a sardonic shadow, and to listen
to the guttural talk of this Greenlander with his old-
fashioned speech and tales of strange things.

They had soon left the crowd behind them. There
were only grazing cattle here, and then, suddenly, they
saw two men coming toward them.

"Norse, by their height," said Thorvald.

The men turned out to be Ulf, with Benedikt Karlsson, out to stretch their long legs. Thorvald invited
them to join in the hunt, "If Paul Knutson will not
wonder where you are."

"Let him wonder," said Ulf. "Benedikt, you are a
Swede and a King's Man. Can you not write a rune on a
rock by the path so that someone will let Paul know
that we are gone?"

"I'm no clerk," said Benedikt.

Olav flushed. "I can write a little," he said modestly.

"Here is a flat rock by the path, then." Thorvald knelt down and drew out his fine steel and tinder box and, sheltering the newborn flame from the wind, soon had a branch of dwarf willow charred enough for writing.

"Use that and when it will write no more, I shall have another for you."

Two or three cows, filled with animal curiosity, drew near, and Smyrill sat down, looking off into the distance toward a rocky islet from which came the distant dog-like bark of seals.

While the others waited, Thorvald whiled away the time with riddles.

"Do you know the questions Blind Gest put to Heidrek?"

Ulf said in his offhand manner, "Try us, Greenlander. If the Norseman cannot answer, perhaps the Swede can."

> *"Four are walking,*
> *Four are hanging,*
> *Two showing the way,*
> *Two keeping dogs off;*
> *One lags behind*
> *All his days.*
> *That one is always dirty."*

"Well, Ulf?" said Benedikt.

"Give me time, give me time."

"If you were a hawk, you would already have missed your kill."

"Well, then, Swede, you tell the answer."

"Certainly, my friend. I may not be a Norwegian but, at least I know the old tales, and am not to be outwitted by a Greenlander, eh, Thorvald?"

"Get on with your answer," gibed Ulf, "or we shall think you are earning time with your tongue."

"I would scorn to. Here you are. So Heidrek replied in the old story:

> " '*A cow is that beast*
> *Which thou didst see*
> *Walk on four feet,*
> *Four teats hang,*
> *And horns defend her;*
> *Her tail hangs behind.*' "

Ulf gave a bray of laughter. He was a noisy young man, seldom lowering his voice. Eirik grinned, and though Olav, bent on his work, did not smile, his eyes looked amused. On many a winter's evening by the fire, he had listened to his father and the men of Hestnaes asking and answering such riddles.

Now he wiped his sooty hands along the turf, and got to his feet.

"Finished already?" asked Benedikt with his negligent good humor. "What have you written, Olav?"

"I have made it short," said Olav, trying to conceal his pride. " 'Benedikt and Ulf hunt with Thorvald of Brattahlid.' "

"All is said in few words," said Thorvald. "Come, then. We shall row up to the head of the fiord and go to the place of one of my farmers, on a lake back from the shore. Egil will put us up and give us horses to bring back the meat. We are sure to find reindeer at the edge of the snow."

They reached Egil's farm after a hard row and a steep climb of several hours along a barely visible path. Olav held Smyrill's collar until the fierce farm dogs had been called back and tied up. The farmer and his wife knew nothing of the ship's arrival, so remote were they; and the presence of the tall strangers frightened the little children of the place, who hid behind their mother like young foxes. Here everything had a rough air. The farm buildings were of stone, but without wooden paneling in the rooms; the cattle seemed smaller and shaggier than at Gardar; and the people had a more savage air, with uncombed hair and garments of frieze, unevenly woven. But after their first astonishment, they welcomed Thorvald and the others hospitably, bringing out coarse bear's meat and bowls of sour milk, and a horn of black crowberry wine, of which the Norwegians had not tasted before. The view from the house was very fine. The land sloped greenly down to a small lake, reflecting both the sky and the white peaks which circled the farm on three sides. Although the snow lay so near, the mountains kept the wind off, and it seemed warmer here than by the fiords. There was not another house to be seen, not a thread of smoke even, nor could the people at the farm hear another human voice calling in the distance, except when a rare visitor climbed to them— and that might not happen twice in a year. They lived by themselves in an uninhabited world: tiny creatures who had held their own for generations in this pocket of the mountains and the ice.

Thorvald went aside to speak with Egil. Olav, who was nearest, heard something said about reindeer and two horses. Then Thorvald dropped his voice. Egil answered, apparently in protest. "It is not lawful," Olav thought he heard the man say, but Thorvald spoke quickly and urgently, and Egil seemed to yield, although unwillingly. By the time they had finished eating, the horses had been caught, and empty packs, stiff with old blood, were strapped to their backs, and halters slipped over their furry heads.

"We shall bring back all they can carry," Thorvald promised. "I have my spear, but you four have only your swords. Egil, what spears have you?"

The man could furnish three rough-looking weapons, the points ground down, but still serviceable. Much to Olav's unspoken dissatisfaction, he was not given one of the spears. He might have claimed Eirik's, but could not bring himself to take away the man's pleasure. Leaving Egil and his family behind, they set themselves again to climbing. There were many little flowers among the rocks, and small birds sprang up from underfoot. A fox looked at them from a distant hillside, slipping away from sight as Smyrill leaped off in pursuit.

They had climbed and walked among the high hill valleys for a long time without coming on any trace of game. The sun had begun its slow, downward curve and Thorvald had spoken of turning back, but seeing the disappointed looks of his guests, had laughed and said they would go on for another hour. Yet when that hour was done, they still went on. Although Thorvald still set the pace as briskly as ever, the others' sea-accustomed legs were beginning to lag, and it was with aching muscles and gasping breath that they followed the short tireless figure ahead of them.

Suddenly Smyrill, at Olav's side, uttered a low warning growl. The dog was scenting the breeze, turning his head this way and that, rumbling softly in his deep throat.

Thorvald looked at him and pointed to the rise ahead, laying his finger to his lips, and again led the way, walking with added caution. He was the first to reach the top, and the others, anxiously watching, saw him smile back at them and nod with satisfaction.

The game had been sighted, but what game it was! They had expected the reindeer, with which they were acquainted, but these creatures were quite different. There were thirty-five or forty of them scattered about, grazing on grasses, lichens and scrub willows in the hollows. They were horned oxen of some sort, short and heavy with thick skirts of hair, nearly sweeping the ground. Five or six calves followed their mothers. As the men watched, one of the cows must have caught their scent in a flaw of wind, for she raised her head and looked toward them, and began to paw the ground angrily.

"Quick!" cried Eirik. "They will run. They have seen us."

"They will not run," said Thorvald. "Olav, if you wish to keep Smyrill alive, you had best hold him by the collar and never let go. These are not reindeer, no, not these," and he chuckled as he began crashing carelessly downhill toward the animals, which had now all taken the alarm and were quickly forming a circle, standing heads outward with the calves in the center. Even the cows were horned, and the circle of heavy matted heads, thick hair-protected chests and savage upsweeping horns looked formidable enough. The bulls were stamping and rubbing their heads against their forelegs, and as the men came nearer they could smell the thick odor of musk rising from them.

Eirik laughed aloud.

"You show us good hunting, Greenlander," he said. "I can see that these are fighters. How do we advance, Captain?"

Smyrill was pulling at the collar, yet when Olav spoke

to him, he obeyed and held back, shivering with excitement.

"Whatever happens, hold your dog, Olav," Thorvald warned again. "Stay with the horses, well away. They stand so, but now and then, a bull will charge out. Heavy as they look, they are as quick as cats on their feet; if they can, they will gore and trample a man with their broad hoofs."

How hateful to be a boy, ordered to keep out of a battle and forced to be a watcher! But for Smyrill's sake, Olav did not protest. Besides, he knew that there was no spear for him. He listened while the others chose a young bull on the far side of the circle to attack. The strong odor of musk, the pawing and rumbling of the oxen, the whining of Smyrill under his hand, the snorting of the horses behind him—all excited Olav almost unbearably. Then the four men, still led by Thorvald, advanced on the animals, and the excitement increased. Olav could see that the bulls' eyes had turned blood-red. Their threatening bellow deepened. Then, with a shout, the hunters ran forward toward the bull they had chosen. Thorvald's spear went home, and then Eirik struck, so deeply that he could not draw the spear out again, though Olav saw him jerking at the haft.

Before Ulf or Benedikt could get their blows in, the wounded bull charged, his head held low to the ground. As Thorvald said, he launched his unwieldly mass of hair and horn forward with astonishing speed. The men scattered before him, the three with spears turning to take up their stands, their right hands flung up to drive the spearheads home if the bull approached them. Eirik ran on, his spear being in the bull's shoulder, and Olav saw that he was laughing at the sport. He was running toward Olav, well ahead of the bull which had turned aside at Thorvald's taunting shouts.

Then everything happened at once. Eirik caught his foot and stumbled forward. At that moment, a second bull, the largest of the bellowing and attentive circle, charged out from his position near by, his upsweeping horns held low. Eirik, who had half scrambled to his feet, dropped flat upon the ground, realizing that he had no time to draw his sword. The other men were at a distance and engaged with the wounded bull. Seeing Eirik's danger, Ulf did indeed break clear and started running and shouting toward him, but he was too far away to be of any help.

All happened in a moment, and in that moment, Olav loosed his hold on Smyrill's collar and, as the big dog shot forward, made a choice upon which Eirik's life hung, and drew his light dagger instead of his sword. Where every second counted, he stood still, balancing the dagger, shifting into the thrower's balance. Then, with all his strength, he threw and, without waiting to see whether he had missed or struck home, sprang down the hillside after Smyrill.

Chapter 6

"She Is a Soothsayer"

T HE DAGGER in itself was not enough to stop the charging musk ox, though it sheared through the heavy mane of the creature's neck and into the flesh. The sudden unexpected pain made the bull pause to see where this enemy had sprung from, and in that moment's pause, Smyrill leaped upward and seized him by an upper ear, hanging on to the one vulnerable place in all that matted body. The bull tried to shake off the dog; not only the pain but Smyrill's weight delayed him. Yet he was still aware of his original purpose, still intent on reaching the prostrate figure of Eirik on the ground. But as he started forward again, dragging

Smyrill with him, Olav reached the spot, and, leaping over Eirik, stood waiting his attack with drawn sword. While Ulf ran up panting, and Eirik scrambled to his feet, the bull charged Olav, who jumped to one side and got his sword into the hairy neck, not far from where the hilt of his dagger still showed. But at the same moment, the bull swept at him with his sharp upcurving horn. Smyrill's weight weakened the thrust but, even so, one horn ripped along Olav's chest and right shoulder. The wounded beast would have followed up his advantage if Ulf's spear had not struck from the other side into his throat. Eirik leaped, shouting, to the fight, and Olav, bleeding as he was, changed his sword into his left hand and struck again. The battle was not for long, though it was furious while it lasted, and Smyrill barely escaped being crushed when the musk ox at last fell. Thorvald and Benedikt came running up, wiping their swords.

"How do you like our Greenland musk oxen? Are they not good fighters?" Thorvald asked. "What, my Olav, has he scratched you? Let me see."

"It is nothing," said Olav. But he let Eirik and Thorvald look at the wound and tie it up with strips torn from his cloak.

"You had best ride one of the horses," said Thorvald. "You will be dizzy from losing so much blood, though luckily the wound is not deep."

"I shall walk," said Olav.

"What were you doing, Eirik? Pretending to be asleep!" Ulf jested. "I noticed as I was running that you looked very comfortable."

"It's more than I felt, then," said Eirik. "But I thought I would rather be trampled than gored."

"An ox has been known to snuff at a man who did

not move and to go away without hurting him." Thorvald looked about him. "Now how shall we get rid of the rest of these fellows? We can't have them looking on while we cut up the carcasses. Another bull, smelling the blood, might charge us while we were at work."

The herd still held its circle, stamping and bellowing uneasily. The men waved at them, flapping their cloaks and shouting, but not a musk ox broke the ring. Thorvald again lighted a fire. The hunters made torches of dry twigs and ran upon the cattle, waving the flames almost in their faces. At last the circle broke, and the herd made off at great speed, the calves as quick on their feet as their padded mothers.

"What a quantity of clothes they wear!" Benedikt exclaimed. "They would never do for court. It spoils their figures," and the men laughed, turning back to the work at hand.

Olav sat down on a rock and watched them, with Smyrill at his feet. There was a ringing in his head and he felt dizzy, and the wound ached and throbbed. But he was happy. For the first time in his life he had faced actual death, and he had neither flinched nor fumbled before it. He and Smyrill together had saved Eirik, and there was a difference in the way the others looked at and spoke to him. Eirik had said when he came to see the wound, "That was like Sigurd's son!" Olav felt the battle merriment still flooding him. For the wound, he cared nothing. Men were not troubled for wounds. The shadows of the hill on which he sat loomed high on the opposite mountains now that the sun was so low, and the snow of their summits seemed more dazzling than ever. It was growing cold. Though noon had been warm, by night there would be hoarfrost again. Olav drew his torn cloak closer about him and sang to himself,

"It is better to be merry
Than to be downhearted,
Whatever may come to hand."

When the little horses had been loaded with meat,
the hunters turned back toward Egil's farm. Now their
going was mostly downhill and often they could see the
bright sparkle of the sea below them and the red path-
way of the setting sun across the waters.

"Somewhere beyond the horizon lie the Lands of
Flat Stones, and of Woods, and of Wine," said Thorvald, once when they stopped to rest. "Somewhere the
people of the Western Settlement are lighting their
cooking fires, if they are still alive."

After the first hour's walking, Olav began to stumble,
and he was forced to accept Eirik's help and to lean
with increasing heaviness upon the man's shoulder.

But he was still in high spirits when at last they
reached the farmstead by the little lake, and Eirik
helped him to a seat by the fire. The woman brought
hot water and ointment, and clean white cloths, but
Eirik would let no one but himself dress the wound,
while the others recounted the events of the hunt. Olav
found it was good to hear himself praised. After the
years of shame, it was good to have proved his courage
among men, and he smiled as Eirik probed at the wound.

Egil's wife and oldest daughter, a thin, half-grown
dwarfish girl, had been busy bringing in ale and fish,
and bowls of blueberries which the children had gathered while the men were away. It seemed strange to
Olav, drowsy by the fire and not very hungry, that no
one sat in the high seat. Surely that was the master of
Brattahlid's place, but Thorvald did not take it. After
they had begun to eat, there was a knock at the door

and a woman entered. For a moment Olav thought that
she must be Norwegian, for she was taller than any
Greenlander they had seen. But from her speech, he
soon saw that she was an islander. Everyone seemed
greatly surprised at her entrance.

"Gudrid! What are you doing here? It is long since
I saw you," Thorvald exclaimed, but Olav thought that
he was not really surprised. He went to the door and
led the woman in, holding her hand. She was an old
woman, but she was still beautiful—or so Olav thought
—in her blue cloak bordered with embroidery and spar-
kling stones. Her hood was of black lambskin lined with
white cats' fur, and she had cats' fur gloves, and carried
a tall staff with jewels in the brass knob under her hand.

"Those are charms in the bag at her belt," Eirik
whispered. His flat face was expressionless with excitement. "She is a soothsayer. You will see."

Thorvald led her to the high seat, and she sat down
in silence while the women brought a smoking hot dish
and set it before her. Eirik sniffed.

"It is goats' milk porridge, and in it are the hearts of
every kind of animal. That was why our Greenlander
was so careful to take the musk oxen's hearts just now!"

The woman ate in silence. They had brought out a
fine brass spoon for her, and a knife with a handle of
walrus tusk; Egil's wife carried her a horn of crowberry
wine.

No one spoke while she ate. Even Benedikt and Ulf
were silent, though their eyes were dancing with a
curiosity close to amusement. When she had finished
the porridge, the woman looked about her.

"I am come, Thorvald."

"And now that you happen to be here, Gudrid, please
look at these young men who are about to set out in

search of the Western Settlement people, and tell us
what their success will be."

"Why do you wish to know?"

"Have you forgotten that my youngest sister, Ingeborg, the nestling of the family, was married into the
Western Settlement?"

The woman Gudrid turned her eagle's look on each
of the men in turn—on Ulf, the outlaw, on Benedikt,
the courtier, on Eirik, the Lapp, and on Olav, with his
right side swathed in bandages half-hidden by his cloak.

"It is a dangerous business," she said at last. "There
is a law against prophecy."

"The priests will never hear," Thorvald answered her
patiently. "Egil's people are all mine. They will say
nothing. Nor will these travelers who sail the day
after tomorrow."

"It is a dangerous business," the woman repeated, as
though she had not heard. "Let them give me something
if they wish to hear what I have to say."

"I have promised you two ewes," Thorvald began,
but the woman silenced him with a motion.

"If you were forty years younger, I would give you
this ring, and welcome," said Benedikt.

And Ulf took up, "I am an outlaw, Gudrid, and must
guard the little I have."

Eirik said, "My fortune is already told."

But Olav, with his left hand, undid a silver brooch,
set with amethysts, from his cloak.

"I cannot give you the arm ring, for it is a love gift,
mother, but this you may have and welcome."

"You do well," Eirik said in his ear; and then, still in
a low tone, spoke to the others. "Be advised. Follow
Olav's example. She reads the future, yet in some way
makes the future, too."

"Only outlanders, like you, Eirik, still believe such nonsense," Benedikt replied loudly enough. "Begin, Gudrid. I am growing sleepy."

The old woman gave him a level look which, for some reason, silenced him. Then she yawned widely and began to sing. Her voice in singing was not an old woman's voice but seemed strong and sweet. She sang of old things, incantations and charms, calling the spirits to her. Olav understood only parts of her singing. Sometimes the words meant nothing to him, but he heard her sing the song of Odin and began to shiver:

> *"I know that I hung*
> *On the windy tree*
> *Nine whole nights*
> *Wounded with a spear,*
> *Given to Odin,*
> *Myself to myself;*
> *On the tree*
> *Of which no one knows*
> *From what root it comes."*

A wind had risen outside and a chained watchdog howled. At Olav's feet, Smyrill moved nearer and pressed against his knees.

Gudrid yawned and yawned and sang on:

> *"Nine songs of might*
> *I learned—*
> *Then I became fruitful*
> *And wise;*
> *I grew and I throve;*
> *Word followed word*
> *With me;*
> *Act followed act . . ."*

Something seemed sighing on the roof. There was a rustling in the air and footsteps overhead. Olav said a paternoster, yet the singing and sounds went on.

Suddenly the woman fell forward on the table before her, and began to speak in another voice, harsh and strident, as though an entirely different person were talking.

"Not there, not there," wailed the voice, and at its sound the fire which had been blazing brightly, sank down into a whisper of blue flames, and the room was almost in darkness. "Not there," repeated the despairing voice. "No sign, no trace. Beyond? Behind? Behind, then? Oh, the cold! Could it be? Could it? Beware!" The voice grew stronger, rose almost to a scream. "The three red hoods, two most unwillingly worn! Alas! Alas! And yet, and yet?" The words trailed off and the voice became silent. The woman's head on the table began to move from side to side and her hands flattened on the board. Slowly she pushed herself upright in the high seat and gazed about her as though bewildered. She looked much older than when she had entered the room.

"It seems to me I have spoken an ill fortune," she said wearily, "and yet—well, get me to bed. I have no more to say."

Egil's wife led her out, and Egil knelt down and stirred up the dying fire.

Benedikt laughed a shaken laugh, and Ulf said moodily, "Just the same, I wish I had given her a brooch."

"I warned you," Eirik agreed. "For myself, it would make no difference. The morning I left Hestnaes, the bread I broke from the loaf had blood on it. But I am glad that Olav here showed himself more generous."

"I do not like anything about the matter," declared Egil, straightening from the fire. "I told Thorvald that it was not a lucky thing to do, to summon Gudrid here, but he was bent on it."

"I wanted to know about Ingeborg," Thorvald muttered. "Certainly the soothsaying did not have a good sound. And yet she said at the end—'and yet'—as though there might be a good end after all."

"Good or bad," said Benedikt, who had recovered his usual bantering tone. "I must sleep. What with your hills and your air, and your padded cattle, Greenlander, we are all worn out."

It was true. Olav, weak from loss of blood, had already fallen asleep, his head against the wall behind him.

Chapter 7

Vidar, the Outlaw

WHEN, next day on the hunting party's return to Gardar, Paul Knutson saw that Olav was hurt, he turned angrily to Eirik.
"Is this the care you take of the boy?"

Eirik grinned ironically. "It is the boy who takes care of me, Paul Knutson," he replied, and gave a brief account of the incidents of the hunt. When he had finished, Paul made no remark whatever, but gave Olav a strange look, doubtful and searching, and turned away.

They sailed next morning after hearing Mass in the cathedral. All the settlement who could be away from

home were present. There was much exclaiming over
the new small window above the altar, through which
the light shone, making a St. Nicholas in robes of bright-
est scarlet, azure and yellow, forever raising his hand
in endless blessing.

The cargo had all been unloaded; the gifts of raisins
and nuts, wine and flour, knives and scythes had been
made. In return, the Greenlanders had given gifts of
their own; another boat for the ship, stout shoes with
soles made from the hides of the bearded seals, walrus-
hide thongs which would never break, hoods lined with
the ruffs of wolves, smoked fish, barrels of sour milk,
and hogsheads of meat in brine, reindeer, seal and mut-
ton as well as duck and snipe—things useful for a voyage
such as the royal ship was embarking upon.

Paul had made arrangements for a pilot, a middle-
aged, bandy-legged man with one eye, named Simon
Oddson, to go with them. Simon drove a hard bargain
in Norse goods, but he claimed to have been more than
once to Markland and Vinland, and declared that he
knew the course to the Western Settlement as well as
he knew the lines in the palm of his hand. A younger
man might have been better, but the young men were
all off to the Northern Grounds for their season of hunting. Paul had to be satisfied with what he could get,
and, with the fog likely to close in at any moment, he
was glad now—bound for the Western Settlement—to
have a man with him who knew the coast.

At present the summer sun shown brightly on the
scene. As the sail took wind and the small waves whispered again along the sides of the Knarr, Olav, standing
at the rail waving to the people on shore, saw that many
of them were weeping. He guessed that few thought
that the royal ship would ever return.

He looked at the high, ice-hooded mountains, at the gray, rocky shore against which broke the sea, at the blue horizon speckled with the blinding white of ice floes—all so empty of human life, so enormous, so unknown. Only these few hundreds of people, this scant two thousand souls, lived here in one fold of the forbidding land; and now that the Western Settlement was gone, there were not other people anywhere to whom they could reach out their hands.

In desperation they had sent out their own little nailless, anchorless ship for help, and help had come. Now this help was sailing away again after a few days of laughter and fellowship. More than ever before, Olav felt that he would gladly die, if by his death he might serve these Greenlanders. Eirik had been right when he said at Hestnaes that Olav thought more of clearing his father's name than of fulfilling Magnus Eirikson's mission. Olav had then said that the two were one, but only now had they really merged.

All day the ship ran along the coast. There was no fog, only a bright summer's light which shone on the bare islands and inhospitable shores and the changing shapes of the mountains, some of which were flat-topped, some shattered and upflung in shapes of rearing stone and ice. Soon they passed the nunnery on its plain, sailing between the shore and a long island, but they were too far away to see the nuns, though they made out low-lying buildings and a little smoke.

After that, the great landscape was bare of human life. They saw plenty of seals and several times whales spouted not far away. Some of the islands and cliffs along the shore seemed thick with birds, so that they were mantled with wings and harsh with a thousand cries.

In the afternoon, Olav found himself talking for the first time with a young man named Gunnulf Arneson, who told him that he was the younger son of a poor farmer living not far from Bergen. His grandfather's brother, he said, had come out to Greenland and had prospered there, having inherited, through his Greenland wife, a large farm in the Western Settlement.

"Fifteen years ago, word came from my father's cousin, Haftor, bidding my father send out one of his sons, that he should marry Haftor's oldest daughter, Margret, and inherit the farm, for Haftor has no sons. I am one of five brothers. None of the others wished to go. But I always hankered to see Greenland and this girl. She is a little older than I am, and of course she may have married."

"You speak, Gunnulf, as though she were at the Western Settlement still."

"I have thought of her there on the farm for so many years and tried to imagine it! To tell you the truth, when I first saw how little the Greenland women are, I did not know that I wanted to marry such a tiny girl. But I observed them closely and some of them are very pretty. My great-uncle was said to have been a handsome man. His granddaughter may well take after him."

"But now that she has gone?"

"I shall go after her and bring her back, and take over the farm."

"And if Margret is married?"

"I shall take one of her sisters."

"You seem very sure of everything, Gunnulf."

"Have I not planned it since I was a little boy? When our only cow fell ill, I thought, 'Some day I shall have many cows,' and when my eldest brother always took the best of everything, I used to think, 'It will be I, not you, my friend, who some day will be rich.' "

"And so you will make it come true."

"And so I will make it come true," Gunnulf repeated, looking at Olav with obstinate eyes, for though he was a good-looking young man, he was lacking in any flexibility of purpose.

On the third day, Eirik saw smoke rising from the shore and soon after, the lookout at the prow made out a small boat lying off an island. Paul steered to meet it and lowered sail. There was a man and his two sons in the boat, along with the carcasses of several seals.

"The hunting is not good," the older man complained after the first greetings were over. "We need much oil for our fires and lamps for the winter. But with the Skraelings so near, we don't dare go to the Northern Hunting Grounds as usual. The women are afraid."

"How many of you are there?" Paul asked.

"There were four farms on the fiord," the man said. "But the people at two of them have gone. They had relatives in the Eastern Settlement. Now there are only five grown men left here, and the women and children. We are afraid all the time."

"Then why don't you go like the others?"

The man dropped his hand on the body of one of the dead seals and looked away toward the land.

"Our families have been on the farms for three hundred years," he said with a kind of defiance. "We'll hold on a little longer."

One of his sons spoke up, "The others will get tired of working for their relations. They will come back."

"They value their own skins too well for that," said the second son, with a short laugh which had more uneasiness than amusement in it.

"Are there no others between you and the Skrael-ings?" Paul asked.

"None, now that the Western Settlement has gone."

The young man who had laughed now added, "You forget Vidar, the Outlaw."

"Oh, Vidar!" said his father. "But no Christian has exchanged a word with him for ten years. He is a savage fellow, no better than the Skraelings he goes about with. Vidar was outlawed for blasphemy and murder. He lives a day's journey up the coast, with his goats. Men have seen him hunting with the Skraelings at the Northern Hunting Grounds, a thousand miles from here."

Paul gave each of the men a knife, which they received with deep gratitude, and for the women he sent a mirror and some oatmeal cakes. They sailed away, but for as long as the boat was in sight, Olav saw that the three men sat motionless, staring after them.

"I wonder about this Vidar," said Paul. "He alone knows the Skraelings, it seems. No doubt he will be up north, too, like the rest," and the outlaw was forgotten.

Yet late on the fifth day, when they were weary of the head wind which had sprung up, they remembered the man again, for coasting along the shore, they saw the entrance to yet another fiord and a small hut sheltered under a hill and goats grazing.

"By heaven!" exclaimed Paul, "there is smoke! Vidar is at home. We will go calling and stretch our legs a little until this cursed wind shifts."

There was a wharf in the shelter of the fiord, to which a small Norse boat was tied, and there were boats made of skin on the bank. As they were going ashore, a man came down from the hut to meet them. They had seen nothing like him in Greenland. Somehow, in Vidar the old strain had had a sudden flare back to its beginnings, or perhaps his race had not been so long on the island, for he was a big man, taller than any of the men whom he greeted except the Swede, Orm Karlsson, and broader-shouldered than Orm. His hair was not yellow but red, and he was dressed outlandishly, in a skin coat and trousers, with a fur-lined hood down his back.

He gave them a hearty welcome, and yet at the same time he was indifferent, as though he could do well enough without visitors. However, since they were here, he would do what he could to show them hospitality. The hut was too small to hold such a gathering of men, but he seated them in its shelter and shouted something they did not understand. In a few minutes a young, round-faced brown woman, dressed as he was, came out with a pitcher of goats' milk and a horn which she passed from man to man, giggling shyly and trying to hide her face.

"It's a Lapp you have there?" Paul demanded in frank amazement, for indeed the woman looked like such a daughter as Eirik might have. But Vidar shook his head.

"A Skraeling," he said. "I married her three years ago. She is a good enough girl. I do not have to beat her."

Sira Andres, the fat priest, here had a word to say. "You mean that you married her in Christian marriage, my son?"

Vidar gave him a blue stare.

"I have been an outlaw for ten years, Father," he replied. "I could not enter a church if I wished to. I mean I married her in the Skraeling fashion. I gave her father four good wooden tubs and an iron-headed harpoon and he gave me the girl."

The priest clucked disapprovingly.

"I shall have to instruct her in our religion and baptize her and marry you both."

"She speaks no Norse," said Vidar. "It will take you a month at least to instruct her, even with my help. Have you the time, Father?"

Unwillingly the priest gave up the plan.

"When we return, then, you must bring her to me."

Vidar smiled and said nothing. The girl went for more goats' milk, but this time it was sour, for she had used up the fresh milking in the first pitcher.

"Where are the Skraelings?" Paul asked. "Shall we come upon them at the Western Settlement?"

"One can never tell, but I think they are farther north."

"Did they destroy the settlement?"

Vidar shrugged. "Sometimes they boast that they did, and sometimes they say that the people all went away. They are great liars."

"And yet when they say that they killed the people, you still have dealings with them?"

"Why should I care?" the man demanded, good-humoredly. "I am a wolf, an outlaw. They turned me out. I do not care if they were killed or went away. I do not care if the Skraelings are killed or go away." He looked at Paul with grim amusement. "I do not care if you are killed or go away."

There was something daunting about the man's equanimity.

"You are never afraid?"

"What is there to be afraid of?" He snapped his fingers. "Do you mean death? I have seen too much of death to fear him. Hell?" he queried, looking at fat

Sira Andres. "But hell, like God, is everywhere. No more here than in Bergen."

"Some day," said Paul slowly, "the Skraelings will turn upon you and kill you."

Vidar smiled.

"Perhaps. But perhaps not. They say that I am so strong that I can carry a full-grown walrus on my back and a harp seal under each of my arms. You do not believe it? Neither do I. But the point is that the Skraelings believe it. They say that I never close my eyes in sleep. That is not true either, but it is a good thing for them to believe. As it is, we are useful to each other. I make them things which they cannot make, and they hunt and fish for me."

When the wind changed toward sunset, Vidar walked down with them to their boat, and for his hospitality Paul gave him a sword and a piece of fine red cloth for the woman. Vidar thanked him, but he had none of the eagerness over steel that every other man in Greenland had shown. He depended on nothing and no one but himself. He was even indifferent to the blessing which Sira Andres, after some inward hesitation, bestowed upon him. Although he bowed his head, it was clearly only out of courtesy.

"You would find Thor's hammer on that man's dishes!" Eirik murmured to Olav as they beat their way out to sea again. "Such a one must Eirik the Red have been, who, when he was outlawed from Iceland, spent his three years of banishment in exploring this uninhabited coast with a wife and little children, and in an open boat, they say. As for the girl, I tried to speak to her and she to me. We could not understand each other, and yet there was some likeness in our talk,

as there is in our faces. I did not guess that the Skraelings were like Lapps."

Olav could see that Eirik was excited by the en-
counter. He sang songs to himself in his own tongue,
and looked much into the distance, thinking. Olav, too,
standing with Smyrill at his knee again—for the dog
had been left aboard when everyone went ashore—
thought much of Vidar and the Skraeling woman. Un-
bidden, a comparison to Adam and Eve came to his
mind; alone in the world and dressed in skins, they too
had been outlawed from the place of their birth. They
had disobeyed God. Olav wondered if Adam had bra-
zened out his punishment like Vidar. There seemed no
weakness in the man.

On the afternoon of the sixth day they came to the
Western Settlement and went ashore. The cattle and
sheep and goats of which Ivar Bardson had spoken had
vanished away. The pastures were much smaller than
those at the Eastern Settlement and were as lifeless
now as the houses. Some of these stood with open doors,
and the birds had nested against their beams and soiled
the floors. From one house a fox and her cubs ran out,
leaving behind a smell of musty grapes and a litter of
old bones. In some houses the doors had been closed
and all was in order. The gut was unbroken in the
windows. The bowls stood on the shelves and some of
the wooden spoons hung in their place on the wall. In
one house there was a carved cradle and in it a little
wooden horse with a mane and tail of real horsehair,
half pulled out.

But nowhere did they find any mark of violence, or
any message of farewell. As they had been told, there
were no boats, and the bells of the churches were gone.

They went into the church nearest the shore and Sira Andres conducted a Mass. Olav, kneeling, thought that he had never felt the presence of God nearer than in that deserted church, with a bird flying in and out through one of the broken windows and the sound of the sea beating on the shore heard in all the pauses of the Latin words.

No one wanted to sleep at the Western Settlement, though there the bedsteads stood, curtained still, and along the walls stretched the cushioned benches for the common men. The place was haunted, whether its former inhabitants were alive or dead. And yet no one was quite willing to go away. Somewhere there must be a message, some clue as to where the people had gone. Paul Knutson and the others lingered until almost dark, searching all the houses within walking distance of the shore, and then at last in the late evening, they wearily climbed aboard and anchored a little out from shore.

No one had much to say. A depression had settled on them all. Only Gunnulf talked of the farm which was to be his. He had recognized the house from the description, with carvings of men under the eaves, halfway up a hill facing south. He talked on and on about it until Ulf told him to be still.

"Wait until you have found your bride, bridegroom. Does love tell you which way to look?"

In the morning Paul decided to go ashore for one more day's search, but Olav got permission to go with Eirik and Smyrill in one of the ship's boats to an island he saw lying off from shore. There he could see landings and drying sheds and fishhouses, just as in Norway, and there even seemed to be a boat pulled up on the beach. If so, it was the only boat they had seen anywhere, but Paul said it was probably a rock.

Olav's wound was much better, but still he left the rowing to Eirik. Few men could have handled the boat alone with such ease as the Lapp showed. Olav sat at the bow, watching the island grow nearer.

"Eirik, it *is* a boat! and someone has left oars leaning against the bank! Someone is still there, Eirik! Look, the door is open. Someone is there! Hurry! He can tell us where they went."

Eirik rowed no faster.

"Is your someone alive or dead, my Olav?" he asked. "In either case, he will wait for us."

Chapter 8

The Sign

WITH SMYRILL at his heels, Olav jumped out the moment that the boat's bow grated on the sand, leaving Eirik to fasten it in any way he pleased. The thing he had seen was no rock but a Norse boat and there were indeed oars. The island was sweet with some small herb growing in the close turf underfoot and the sun shone on the rocks, making them sparkle as though they were scattered with bits of jewels. The little paths ran from the shore to the fishhouses and to the cabin, and were all clearly marked. Surely they were still being used! Yet Olav, climbing up from the beach, did not like the fact that there were no split codfish drying on the shakes and along the clean rocks, and no smoke oozing out between the cracks of the smokehouse.

Still he hurried on, with Smyrill now running ahead. There could be many reasons why a man might not be fishing just then. The boy, too, was almost running and his heart was pounding, partly with the speed at which he was climbing the steep path, but more with expectancy and an anxiety which struggled with his soaring hope. Suddenly Smyrill ran back to him, looking uncertain and whimpering uneasily.

Then at last Olav saw the master of the island. He was lying face downward before the door, and one arm in its frieze sleeve was stretched out at right angles to his body. His hood had fallen back and it was not a man's head that showed in the sunlight, but a white skull. Olav went forward and knelt down, saying the prayers for the dead, and soon Eirik came and knelt beside him, his voice joining with Olav's.

"See," the Lapp said when they were done. "He has a knife in his hand."

Olav looked more closely at the skeleton fingers and true enough, there was a knife beneath them, but such a knife! The blade was scarcely four inches long, worn with countless sharpenings. It was bent, too, so that it must have been a weak defense for the man when he made his last stand against the door of his house.

"There are two heaps of stones on the beach above high-tide mark. If my guess is right, they are Skraeling graves. Even with that knife, he did not die alone, but as a man should," said Eirik.

"He must have stayed on when the others left."

"Like Vidar."

"But this one was a little man."

"Yes. When the Skraelings came to see why there was no smoke from the settlement, they found him here. And, finding him alone, they killed him."

"The last man of the Western Settlement."

The two stood for a moment more looking down at the thing at their feet, then Eirik said with a sigh, "There is a wooden shovel by a shed. I will dig a grave. See if you can find his other arm. Then we will go for Paul Knutson and Sira Andres. I suppose he was a Christian, at least he has marked a cross over his door."

With Smyrill's help, Olav found the skeleton forearm and hand down by one of the fishhouses where some fox must have dragged it. Several fingers were missing, but he brought it back and placed it beside the body. Later, when Sira Andres came with Paul and Orm Karlsson, Nicolas Byrgeson and half a dozen more, the priest looked long at the man.

"How is the upper left arm placed, my son?" he asked Eirik.

"Out from the body, like the right."

"Would you say that that was a natural way for a man to die?"

"No," said Eirik. "I begin to understand."

Nicolas Byrgeson pressed forward, his ugly face alight with a kind of joy.

"He died like a penitent, Sira Andres! He died making with his own body the sign of the cross."

"Though he died unshriven, with his sins upon him, yet surely he is today in heaven," said the priest.

Nicolas took the valuable cloak from his shoulders, not even removing the amethyst brooch which held it. "Let my cloak be honored by shrouding him," he cried.

So they buried the man in Nicolas' cloak, in the grave

that Eirik had dug, and Sira Andres, with his own hand, made a cross and carved on it "The Last Man of the Western Settlement," for they did not know his name.

That night, once more on shipboard, anchored in the entrance of the fiord, it was long before Olav slept. This empty barren place, guarded by one skeleton, oppressed his spirits. Awake as he was, he could hear his companions tossing and sighing to themselves, each man perhaps wondering what his business was here at the ends of the earth.

The next morning Paul gave the order to sail for the islands to the west. Simon, the pilot, wished to set the course for Helluland, the Place of Flat Stones. Here the Greenlanders usually stopped for water on their way to Markland, where the forests grew.

"They would run out of water," said Simon. "There must have been nearly eight hundred people, and they have only the boats we use for the Northern Hunting Grounds, which usually carry about thirty men. But add cows and sheep and goats, let alone women and children and household gear! If they got twenty people into a boat, they would be lucky!"

He began to count busily on his fingers and announced his conclusion.

"They must have started off with forty boats at least, many more than Eirik the Red brought back with him from Iceland in 986. Eirik started with twenty-five, but only fourteen ever reached Greenland. My ancestors came out a little later with Thorbjorn Vifilsson. Their ships were larger in those days than the ones we are able to build. I think our Western Settlement people could not have taken much stock with them—just the best and enough to begin again somewhere."

What a bleating and lowing there would have been
from one boat to another, Olav thought. Surely the
seals and the whales must have been astonished! If they
could only ask that whale, now blowing his fountain
of spray not a hundred feet from the Knarr, *he* could
have told them which way the Greenland ships had
gone. But men had lost the art of understanding the
speech of birds and animals as in the old tales. The seals
might bark directions to them, but neither Simon nor
Paul nor even Eirik could tell what they said.

A fog was coming in, veiling all the stony slopes and
the small green fields of the Western Settlement. Only
the white indifferent mountaintops shone above the
long veil of mist. All day the people in the ship could
see them dropping lower and lower on the horizon, but
the next morning they were gone.

Some days later they came to the wild and barren
shores of Helluland, where the sea complained forever
against the granite cliffs, and the sea birds seemed the
only inhabitants. Here Simon proved himself a skilful
navigator, for after coasting for two days along rocky
promontories, he brought the ship into a small harbor.
Climbing over the great flat stones which formed the
shingle, they did indeed find a spring which flowed out
from under a rock and made a channel down to the sea.

But there was no least sign that the Greenlanders
had been there, though Smyrill nosed at a footprint in
the damp earth at the lip of the water.

"Skraeling," said Simon, shaking his head, "This was
not made by one of our people."

So they filled their water barrels and sailed south
again. After being delayed by head winds and fog they
came to a land covered with green trees. Once again
Simon showed his skill by bringing them into a long

cove where they found old cabins and many stumps of trees and a platform to help in getting the logs aboard ship.

"I was here ten years ago—no, eleven," said Simon. "I think no one has been here since. But they wanted new timbers for the bishop's hall and we came."

"Did you build these cabins?" Paul asked.

But Simon said no. Other Greenlanders had built them long ago. His party had added only the lean-to shed over there and repaired the landing stage.

Again there were no signs of the lost colony and a consultation was held. Simon spoke up for returning to the Eastern Settlement.

"These are the known steps to Vinland," he said. "If they had gone to Vinland, they would surely have stopped here, even if they did not stop for water at Helluland. There is nothing more to be done in this direction, and winter is coming on."

But Paul insisted upon going to Vinland.

"They may have met with stormy weather and have been driven off the land. But everyone knows that Vinland is a rich place, with a mild climate. At Bergen and at the Eastern Settlement alike, it was agreed that they would have gone to Vinland."

Simon shrugged and his one eye looked obstinate and resigned.

"I am here to obey your orders, Paul Knutson, but we should be much better off this winter at Gardar, and in a week or ten days it will be too late to change your intentions, even if you should then want to."

Some suspicion crossed Orm Karlsson's mind.

"Have you ever been to Vinland? Will you swear to it on the cross?"

The pilot looked uncomfortable and tried to laugh.

"Perhaps not quite so far."

"Have you been any farther than this? Come, speak up, man!"

"Well, no, since you insist."

Orm turned to Paul. "This is how the Norwegians choose their pilots!"

But Paul made light of it.

"Simon will get us to Vinland without difficulty. He is a good navigator, even if somewhat of a liar."

"Between you, the whole voyage will be bungled," Orm snapped, but he said nothing more.

They stayed for five days in Markland, hunting deer and bear for fresh meat, then set sail again, passing along a changing coast, sometimes rugged and menacing, sometimes inviting them with long white beaches. And as they sailed on, the dark green forests changed slowly until many of the trees had leaves. At first these leaves were green or greenish-yellow, but became more and more golden in color, until they lighted up the coast in pale yellows and scarlets, more brilliant than the finest robes worn at court.

The weather, which had been squally and wet, turned bright and dry and there were only light winds, mostly from the northwest. At night the moon seemed mild and enormous, rising out of the sea.

"If this is Vinland, it is indeed Vinland the Good," said Olav to Eirik. "I have never seen such a fine land— no, not even Norway can compare with this."

"It is a good land," said Eirik, "but I miss the white of snow at this time of year."

To Smyrill's great delight, they often went ashore in sheltered places, looking always for some mark to show them that people had been there before them, for surely the Greenlanders would have built shelters where they landed. But they never found anything except that once, back among some trees they came upon an old cap-shaped hut, made of birch bark, laid upon propped-up sticks.

"These must be a different kind of Skraeling," said Simon. "I hope we meet with none of them. It has always been because of the Skraelings that our people have left Vinland."

The leaves were falling from the trees, turning the earth bright under the bare branches, when they came at last to the longest beaches they had ever seen. Here they followed the land westward and, passing by the roar of the waves upon the sand, came to a sheltered bay, where they dropped anchor.

"What is that?" asked Paul, who was standing in the bow, looking intently landward. "Are those not buildings there, back a little from the shore?"

Simon was more excited than the others had ever seen him.

"These are no work of Skraelings," he exclaimed, squinting ahead with his one eye. "They never use hewn timber. Either we have found some trace of our friends or these are Leif's houses, built by Leif the Lucky himself."

On nearer view, the houses, though solidly built, were found to be very ruinous. It was clear that they had more than once been patched up and rebuilt by later comers, the last time perhaps not more than thirty years before.

Simon had no idea who might have been there last.

"Sometimes in the old days, when our boats were better, the people who went to Markland for lumber would coast southward for a ways, some farther than others. We do not remember who they were, for there is no saga about their adventures as there is about Leif's."

The group spent the winter at Leif's Houses, once more repairing the old haunted buildings that Leif had raised so long ago. He had been the first white man to live at Vinland and here his foster father, the German Tyrker, had found the grapes from which the name had come.

Olav, whose wounds were healed, whistled to Smyrill and went off hunting for grapes, too, which he found at last on leafless vines. They had felt the touch of frost and had little flavor. All that was left on most of the branches were the skeleton stems, and yet here and there a dark purple globe still hung and he ate them eagerly. He had tasted raisins often enough at the king's house, but now for the first time he saw the living fruit. This was a rich land, beautiful and kind. Game was plentiful; and so were the streams and springs of clear water. To men accustomed to Norway and Sweden, even the coldest weather here seemed nothing to speak of, and the snows, when they came, never lay long on the ground.

By now, no one had much hope of finding the lost Greenlanders here, yet Paul took half the men and sailed on several excursions up and down the coast looking for traces which were not there. Olav and Eirik went once, but usually they were glad enough to stay at Leif's Houses and go fishing or hunting.

One day when the weather stood between winter and spring, with old wet leaves underfoot, the smell of earth in the air and the last snow on the north sides of the trees dwindling to nothingness, Olav and Eirik took Smyrill and went hunting. The supply of sour milk and cheese was running low and so large a company needed a good deal of fishing and hunting to supply them. Olav and Eirik preferred the woods, but on this day the hunting had not been good, and they had sighted nothing but a rabbit or two.

"We will go as far as the spring we once found," said Eirik. "Then we must return or we shall be overtaken by the darkness and there is no moon."

They were moving very quietly, hoping to find deer or perhaps a bear at the spring, when suddenly Eirik, who was in the lead, stiffened, and looked warningly for a second over his shoulder. Holding Smyrill by the collar, Olav crept closer, and saw a figure in the small glade before them. It was a man, bending above the water, drinking. He was dressed in a deerskin, worn with the hair inside and red and yellow decorations on the outside hide. Two fine ermine skins made bracelets about his dark upper arms, and there seemed to be disks of copper or gold in his ears. He was certainly not at all like Vidar's wife.

None of the watchers had moved, but perhaps their intent stare was enough to warn the stranger, for suddenly he seized the bow beside him and slipped into the thicket so smoothly that scarcely a twig vibrated. They had a glimpse of a tall lean body, and of hair so black that it shone for a moment, white in the shaft of sunlight, as a crow's wing will do when the bird flies up.

Then the man was gone, and Eirik and Olav were left to stare at each other. They did not speak until they were nearly home. Then Eirik said, "Surely that man had the look of a fighter."

In the next few days, before Paul returned from coasting along the shore, Olav several times had the feeling that he was being watched from the woods. And

Orm, the Swede, who had been left in charge, set a watch and gave orders that the men were to hunt not less than six together, and that at night they were to sleep with their arms beside them.

But as no more Skraelings were seen, the alarm died down, though the affair added to a restlessness which had been increasing among the men ever since the wind had turned into the southwest.

The easy winter softened to spring. One night, half asleep on their furs along the wall benches, they heard through the smoke vent the calling of the great geese passing northward overhead. Each day the small leaves were greener in the thickets and more unseen animals scuttled in the underbrush.

Then one day, after they had eaten, a bird sat on the ridgepole of Leif's hall and sang for a long time.

Paul listened, staring through the open door at the sea.

"It is spring now," he said, when the bird was silent. "It is time for us to return."

"Yes, it is time," said Orm, who sat near by, "but where are we to go, Paul? I have been meaning to ask you what was in your mind."

Paul found and played with the hilt of his dagger.

"I have given the matter much thought," he said almost unwillingly. "We are all convinced that the Greenlanders never reached the coast of these lands. I can only believe that a storm came up, and that, over-crowded as they were, their boats were lost."

Benedikt Karlsson, beyond on the doorstep, slapped his hand against his knee.

"Come, come, Paul!" he said, half laughing. "Who would believe that all forty or fifty of the boats could be wrecked? Some would have survived. Fourteen of

Eirik's twenty-five got to Greenland—cattle, sheep, wives, children, spinning wheels and all."

Paul flushed.

"They may have met with a mighty storm."

"No one in Greenland spoke of any storm of particular violence."

"I can see no other explanation. They have vanished. What is there left for us to do that we have not done?"

The others looked at him nonplused. A few men had gathered to listen to the talk of the leaders and now several of them exclaimed, "Let us go back to Bergen. We have done all that we could."

But Paul paid no attention to them, waiting, his eyes fixed on Orm. When the Swede did not speak, he said, "Well, have you no suggestion?"

Nicolas brayed, "The king said that we were to find them."

Paul shrugged his shoulders impatiently.

"We cannot find them under the sea."

Olav, who had been sitting beside Benedikt at the door, remembered Gudrid the soothsayer at Egil's house, and the voice which was not Gudrid's voice saying, "No sign—no trace. Beyond? Behind? Behind, then?"

Hardly knowing what he said, he exclaimed: "We must go behind Vinland!"

The leaders swung on him in amazement.

"What are you saying, Olav?" Paul demanded. "What boy's foolishness is this?"

Olav had no answer. A look of uncertainty came into his dark eyes, but he repeated, "Behind Vinland."

"Bah!" said Paul, turning away, wasting no further words. Now one-eyed Simon, the Greenland pilot, spoke up out of the shadows of the ruinous room.

"I'm a fool to spoil my own chances for going home this summer, but the boy is right. There *is* a way to get behind Vinland."

No one slept late on the royal ship. Very early, after the night only a few hours long, when the first light streaked the sky, the cry came for waking. Yawning and stretching, the men rose and went up on the deck. It did not take many hands for the actual sailing in calm weather. A few men to hoist or lower the great striped sail, someone to spell Simon at the steering oar, and a lookout at the bow—that was all actually needed. The rest played endless games of draughts or told stories of their exploits, enlarging the image each had of himself for the admiration of his friends, or sang old songs or invented new ones.

Olav was not alone in feeling an exhilaration in finding himself once more in a place of ice and cold sunlight. The bright blue sea, the floes on which they sometimes caught a glimpse of a white bear and her cub, the towering icebergs hiding caverns as blue as flowers under their jagged heights—all these filled the men with elation. The coast was a thing of ice and rock again; they had to beware of jagged reefs, and mountainous snowy islands and the long underparts of the bergs; they moved among fangs of ice and stone. Every man was glad to be back in the north again. If they had been bound for Greenland, they would by now have set their course to the eastward, but they had instead sailed westward past a jagged point and an island, and were now headed again southward. So far all had gone well.

"If the old tales of Thorfinn Karlsefni's voyage are true," Simon had said that spring day at Leif's, "we will come to a land of trees, and then, sailing north and ever westward, we shall come to a land of tundra and snow. Then, keeping that land on our right, we shall come to Hóp, where a river flows past sandbars into the sea. There Karlsefni found good pasturage for the cattle he brought with him, and built a settlement; there his wife, Gudrid, who had been the widow of one of Leif's brothers, bore him a son, Snorri, the first child born in the western islands."

"If this Karlsefni was content with the place, why did he leave it?" Paul had demanded.

"You know how it is. There was quarreling, and they had trouble with the Skraelings. One man, the old hunter, Thorhall, whom they called crabbed and quarrelsome, finally went off by himself in one of the ship's boats with nine other men, complaining that he hadn't had a chance to find grapes and make wine as he had expected. A storm blew them past Greenland and they landed up in Ireland, where they were seized upon as thralls. There's never been any love lost between us and the Irish."

"Was this man, Karlsefni, a Norwegian or a Greenlander?" someone else had asked.

"Neither. He was from Iceland, but his wife, Gudrid, a fine woman by all accounts, had married in Greenland. My own people originally came to Greenland with her father in the early days. Everyone knows the story of Karlsefni's voyage. It is true, they all went back to Iceland in the end, but they stayed in Hóp for three years, and when they stopped in Greenland, they had nothing but praise for the place. When things go wrong with any of us, we say, 'If my fate doesn't get better, I'll sail off to Hóp.' "

"And this is behind Vinland?" Paul had insisted.

"As the boy says. From the sailing directions, it must

be behind Vinland, though perhaps Hóp is not so far
south. Probably Karlsefni, finding a suitable spot, did
not sail as far south as he might have done. But if the
Western Settlement people didn't go to Vinland—as
they clearly didn't—they must have chosen Hóp, as
nearer to them."

Paul had frowned.

"Why could they not have left a message as to their
plans?" he groaned.

Everyone had asked that question at one time or
another, and the only answer to it seemed to be that
some word *had* been left at the shore, and that the
Skraelings had taken it. Perhaps, if it had been written
on wood, the savages may have burned it in one of
their campfires, of which there had been several traces
on the beach.

In the end, Paul had decided to follow Karlsefni's
route for a week or two westward of the point where it
left the Greenland course.

"You say, Simon, that here, too, there is forest land,
like Leif's Markland?" he had asked, and Simon had
nodded.

"A bear came out of the woods."

"Well, then, as you said on the way to Vinland, these
people, burdened with cattle and households, would
surely have gone ashore at least for water. If in two
weeks we find signs of them, we will go on, in God's
name. If we find no signs, we will turn back to Greenland, while we can still get there this summer, and
admit, as I think, that their boats were lost in a storm.
Are you satisfied with this decision, Orm? And you,
Nicolas?" he had asked the leaders among the Swedes.

Orm nodded his head immediately, but Nicolas asked
time to pray for God's guidance before he gave an

answer. Yet in the end he agreed that unless there were some signs of the lost Greenlanders, there was no point in following a wild-goose chase to its end.

Everyone breathed more easily when Nicolas had spoken, for what he agreed to, Magnus Eirikson, at Bergen, would agree to when the time came.

So here they were in the far north again, set on a new course, the unknown lands once more sliding past their plunging rail, but this time to the east of them. It was early summer and all the ocean birds were beginning to nest along the cliffs, jostling one another and quarreling over the best nesting places. Seals of several kinds were plentiful, and one day they saw several walrus looking at them, enormous solemn creatures with gleaming tusks, most of whose length glimmered faintly from below the clear water.

One evening they entered into a sea of icebergs. It was surprisingly warm. The wind had died down and the water was perfectly smooth. Although it must have been night, the sun still lay on the northern edge of the ocean, and filled the air with brightness, which glowed on the dark rocks of the headlands beyond, and turned the icebergs to pinnacles of flame in the blood-red sea. That evening the seals were numerous, and Ulf suggested that some of the younger men should take a boat and go hunting.

Paul could see no objection. They could always use fresh meat, and he was an experienced leader who had long ago learned to give the men under him as much freedom as seemed wise.

Benedikt, who had struck up a close friendship with the young outlaw, went also, and Gunnulf and a young man named Edvin Sokkeson, and the Swede, Vinalde Algatsson.

"Coming?" Ulf asked Olav. "But don't bring the dog. He may bark at the wrong moment."

"Smyrill knows when to be silent," Olav protested.

"He gets underfoot," Ulf said impatiently. "If you come, it is on my terms. But Eirik, of course, is welcome. It's a night for sorcery."

Ulf was always bold in his speech, the only man who openly called Eirik a sorcerer. There was something wild about him, but likable too; not a man who had the wisdom necessary for leadership, but a good friend in a tight place. He was the handsomest man on the ship, and there were many handsome men on board. Benedikt often said that Ulf could make his fortune at court if he would learn to rule his tongue.

Eirik, like everyone else, humored Ulf.

Now he said, "Smyrill will wait," and gave Olav a hand over the rail.

They killed the first seal in the green shadow of an iceberg, whose crest seemed transparent fire. Somewhere in an unseen valley between its peaks, a lake had formed, and from it the water ran down into the sea in singing cascades. Ulf was excited by the beauty around him. He was facing into the low sun and seemed to be made of gold and dressed in gold, and his quick eyes caught a light of flame which daunted Olav a little.

As they were dragging the dead seal into the boat, a white bear, disturbed by their voices, appeared in the opening of a cavern in the side of the iceberg nearest them, and made as though to take to the water.

Ulf looked up from the dead seal and laughed aloud with pleasure.

"Here is sport! We will bring his skin to Magnus! Row for him, friends! Bend to it!"

For the first time Eirik spoke.

"Softly, Ulf! This is no place for loud voices."

But Ulf was excited and beyond control. The bear stopped, looking toward them, and then took to the jewel-like water.

"Wait, coward!" Ulf shouted exultantly to the vast beast. "Wait!"

But before he could say "coward" a second time, a great side of the iceberg, jarred by the vibration of his cry, broke loose and plunged roaring into the sea not twenty feet from the boat, which rocked sickeningly in the swell and nearly capsized. For minutes the men had all they could do to balance her as wave after wave struck them, and all around them the icebergs complained in their deep caverns and broken archways, and Smyrill howled anxiously from the distant vessel.

When the disturbance had at last quieted down, Ulf turned a rueful face to Eirik.

"Next time I'll take your advice, Lapp. The bear has got away. We'll try for another seal and go back before a second mountain falls on us."

Next morning there was enough breeze for them to leave behind them the iceberg herd. Thereafter they met only small groups, drifting southward and melting as they drifted. After another day's sailing, they began to see stunted trees in the folds of the rocky shore.

"You see, we are coming to the woods," said Simon, relieved. The responsibility of this voyage weighed heavily upon him, and he wore himself out at the steering oar, unwilling to let anyone else take his place, until exhaustion forced him to sleep. Even then he lay on deck, still close to his station, and slept uneasily, rising in a few hours to take the oar again. He never passed Olav without a frowning glance from his good eye, or a resentful word.

"Why did you ever speak, boy?" he grumbled. "How should you have known anything about what lies 'behind Vinland'?"

"Someone in Greenland said the words," Olav replied vaguely.

"Then I wish his tongue had first withered between his teeth."

"It was a woman."

"Even worse, the meddler."

But though Simon, who carried the responsibility, might grumble, Olav was enjoying himself. True, he thought sometimes of Ingrid, and always wore her bracelet on his arm, and sometimes he wondered how his mother was, and how things went at Hestnaes, and if the wild flowers were again in bloom on the sod roofs of its buildings. But this voyage was better than living mewed up at court, doing the same thing day after day. This was the life his father had loved. If only Sigurd might have been here, instead of lying under the sea in the Narrow Straits.

The trees now had grown larger. They were forest trees at last, and the coast had begun to turn westward instead of south. So far the saga of Karlsefni held true. Paul stationed two lookouts at the prow and another two at the stern of the boat to watch the shore for any sign that might indicate that Christians had been there.

"Call out if you see rivers or streams. That's where they'd land."

But though he sent men ashore a dozen times, they found no traces of those whom they sought.

"In two more days we head for Greenland," he said flatly one evening as they ate their suppers, still by daylight. He looked at Orm and Nicolas as he spoke. For the Norwegians he made all decisions, but the Swedes were in a different position. Although Paul was nominally the head of the expedition, they represented the king.

Orm was a sensible man. "You have done all you could, Paul," he said.

Nicolas Byrgeson's ugly mouth was silently moving, like a lean sheep chewing its cud. He was probably praying. Although he was the weakest man aboard, often given to stomach-aches and sneezing, he was bent on this expedition more steadfastly than any of the others.

At last, seeing all eyes upon him, he coughed and sighed.

"I suppose you have done all that the king would expect," he said grudgingly. "Two more days, though. If God wills us to go on, he will send a sign," and Nicolas rose, and calling Sira Andres, who was still very much enjoying his dinner, went on deck with the priest to pray a little apart, under the last rays of the evening sun.

For two more days they sailed westward, sending a boat ashore several times each day where a bay or stream suggested a likely place for landing, but they found no evidence of human life.

Late on the second afternoon, they came upon an island which from end to end was white with birds and canopied with wings.

"Before we begin our return voyage, we had best gather some eggs," Paul said. Everyone wanted to go ashore on the island. They were in a strange mood, glad to be starting on the long voyage home, yet disappointed at having failed in what they had set out to do. Only Simon was completely satisfied. He had given good service, told all he knew without reservation; now he thanked God that he might look forward to seeing his wife and children before the winter settled in.

He anchored the ship in the lea of the island and stayed aboard her with one or two other men. The rest took the boat at the stern and rowed ashore, making several trips of it. The birds made a terrific outcry at their coming and swooped down at the faces of the men, snapping their beaks threateningly as they flew past. But the Norwegians only laughed as they gathered the eggs into their hoods, scattering and climbing and calling back and forth like boys on a holiday.

This time Smyrill had been allowed to come ashore with the others. The steep climbing among the nests held no attraction for him. Wagging his tail gravely, and looking continually back over his shoulder, he coaxed Olav off across a sloping promontory close to the sea, away from the others. A pebbly beach lay beyond it and then another low promontory. This, too, the boy and dog crossed. There were a few birds here which their coming disturbed, but not many. The uproar of men and birds was far behind them. And so they came to the second beach.

And here Olav saw something that changed the course of all their lives. For lying above high-water mark was the hull of a Norse boat. Half the planking, chafed and splintered, still clung to the ribs, and a part of the dragon's head at the bow was in its place. Farther up the beach, a broken oar lay on the shingle above high-water mark, and the wavelets tugged and played with what had been the skeleton of a sheep, now only bones ballasted with sand.

God had sent the sign for which Nicolas Byrgeson prayed.

Chapter 9

Reindeer Valley

WHEN PAUL and the rest of the company had seen the keel on the beach, there was no longer any question of turning back. Only a man named Johan Markusson, a Swede from the king's guard, spoke up for still returning to Greenland. He was one of those men who always take the opposite side of any argument, and that pugnacious habit of mind of his, which had grown increasingly, was hard to put up with. Everyone was tired of hearing his "no" on the heels of their "yes." Now Orm said severely, "It will be well if Magnus Eirikson does not hear of this, Johan," forcing the man into unwilling silence.

Except for Johan, and perhaps a few others who held their tongues, the men were more than willing to be on the now hopeful trail. They crowded for their turn in the boat and, once aboard ship, bombarded Simon with questions. Even Simon caught fire, anxious as he had been to return to the Eastern Settlement that year.

"Can we reach Hóp before the ice closes in?" they kept demanding, and he smiled and shrugged his thick shoulders.

"How can I say? Yes—if the old directions are right, though Karlsefni himself spent a winter to the north. Still it is fairly early in the summer. We may yet sit down with Greenlanders to meat before the snow flies, but I can promise nothing."

"I shall be glad to drink milk again," declared Sira Andres, who relished his food at all times. "How will it seem to be served cheese and butter, my friends? And as soon as the banns have been read, we'll celebrate Gunnulf's wedding to his Margret."

Gunnulf looked embarrassed and pleased at the sudden attention turned upon his affairs, as the men about him jested with him, and Paul promised to save a keg of ale for the marriage feast.

"Do not forget in all these rosy plans," interrupted Nicolas, "that you may be better engaged, Sira Andres, in wrestling for the souls of these misguided people than in feasting with them."

But he could not dampen the carefree enthusiasm around him. Once they came to Hóp and found the new settlement, their troubles would be over. They imagined the welcome such exiles would give them; in that overflowing of hearts, Christ would surely enter in with them and sit at the board. Their quest would be ended in joy.

Up to this time all had been plain sailing for them. True, they had not found the Greenlanders in Vinland, but their winter there had been pleasant and by no means arduous, and in all their sailing up to this time, they had met relatively little trouble from storms or fog.

But now, as though to test their patience when their enthusiasm was at boiling point, nature seemed to turn against them. As they headed north again, having apparently followed the shores of a great bay, with the land to the westward, day after day they encountered fierce head winds and either made little progress or were actually driven back on their course. Food became scarce, and at last Paul was forced to seek shelter behind a headland and send the men out hunting and fishing. The trees by now had become scarce, and game, which had been so abundant, was hard to find. Even the teeming sea seemed reluctant to give up its fish. They were nearly ten days in the place before they had food enough to make it safe for them to go on, and then, the wind having died down, fog took its place. After two more days of enforced idleness, the haze lifted a little and they could see the tops of the promontories and of an island offshore.

"In God's name, let us go on," urged Nicolas, standing with the other leaders near the naked mast.

Looking up, Paul could not see the gilded weather vane cock at its tip. He seemed doubtful.

"What is your opinion, Simon?"

Simon squinted his one eye and stared out into the fog. The roll of breakers, raised by the recent winds, could still be heard on rocks and beaches unseen behind the white vapor, but not far away.

"It might be done," he said at last, "but it would be dangerous sailing."

"Then we will wait."

But Nicolas would not have it so and Orm, swayed by his vehement reliance on God's grace, joined him in urging Paul to let the ship sail.

"There is only a little wind," said Orm. "We can coast along quietly. And already the fog is lifting. I can see nearly a stone's throw from us now."

"Are we to rot here for a little mist," Nicolas cried, "when God's work waits to be done?"

Paul looked out over the swell and truly he could see farther than before. They had not come upon ice for some time.

"I do not like it."

"We will take the responsibility, Paul," Orm urged. "If we are to arrive at Hóp this year, we must get at it."

Two swans flew over the ship, their great wings beating with a loud sound and then their whiteness dissolved in the general whiteness. The fog was breaking up somewhat, and through its floating tatters the blue sky showed. For a moment a faint sunlight shone across the deck and was gone.

"What are you waiting for?" Nicolas once more demanded, bringing his ugly grimacing face close to Paul's. "Will you leave nothing to God? How should harm come to the ship in his service?"

"We are safe in his hand," said Orm.

"Stop urging him, brother," spoke up Benedikt, who as usual was lounging at the rail. "Don't you see that Paul plans to stay here and found a colony of his own?"

Ulf gave one of his loud laughs, "We will milk the wild reindeer, then, and teach the bears to be our servants."

"Fi," Nicolas rebuked the younger man. "This is a serious matter, God's business."

Paul yielded. "I do not like to sail today, but you overrule me." He ordered the great sail hoisted.

The fog, instead of lifting farther, closed in a little more. Paul stationed two of the best men at the bow to listen for breakers ahead and keep a sharp watch for any obstruction, but the reef on which the Knarr ran was submerged just enough so that it could be neither seen nor heard on such a day.

The ship was sailing very slowly; it struck the rock with a delayed grating insistence. Olav was one of those who finally succeeded in pushing it off with oars, while others in the stern boat hawled, and prayed that the walrus hide ropes would hold.

For a little while it was hoped that no damage had been done, but soon the carpenters reported that the vessel was taking in water, and was beyond bailing.

Paul, white-faced, set the course back for the road-stead which they had left a few hours before. Nicolas went to find Sira Andres, to join his prayers with the priest's, but Orm sought Paul.

"This is the fault of us Swedes," he said. "We had not enough patience and overruled you."

Paul laid his hand for a moment on the other's shoulder. "No man can always be wise. The chief fault lies with him who gives the order."

Orm had never spoken to the Norwegian familiarly before, but now he said, "You have a great heart, my Paul."

It was found that the Knarr had to be beached; while they were repairing the rent in her bow, Paul gave orders to scrape all her keel. They were delayed ten days on that beach, and when they went to sea again they had scarcely been gone a week before four of the men came down with an unknown sickness.

Eirik had a gift with such things. If he secretly said
spells over the medicines he gave, while Sira Andres
intoned his prayers, no one questioned him, for the men
began to recover. Then when they were once more able
to come on deck, Toralde Gnupson, one of Paul's
farmer-fighters, had a relapse.

"He is beyond my help," said Eirik, his broad face
worn with fatigue.

The man wanted to die ashore, and Paul would not
refuse him this last request. They anchored in a bay
and carried Toralde in a litter to where the turf began,
spreading the sail from one of the boats above as a
canopy to shield him from the sun. Paul and Sira
Andres and Eirik stayed with him, but the rest were
given permission to do as they liked.

Benedikt and Ulf chose to go fishing, but Olav and
Smyrill were in a mood to explore the inland for a little
way. Eirik would not leave the dying man, whom he
had known well in the days when their masters' ships
had fought the Russian pirates bow to bow.

At first Olav saw scattered figures on the plain that
sloped away from the sea, but they clung to the shore,
and soon he and Smyrill had lost them beyond the
hardly perceptible swells of the plain. The boy had not
brought his spear or arrows with him. There had been
little game along this coast, so he did not trouble to
bring anything but his sword. Stinging flies bothered
him for a while and he thought of turning back, but a
strong breeze began to blow, and the insects became
less troublesome with their buzzing and biting.

Smyrill ran about in an ecstacy of joy at being on
shore again. He was a patient sailor, but had no liking
for shipboard, with its cramped space and its frequent
toss and roll. Now the summer sun shone warm on an

endless plain covered with grass and moss and flowers, where all the cattle of Greenland might have found room to graze. But it seemed empty of animal life. Only butterflies veered above the flowers and now and then birds started up from almost underfoot, and once, indeed, Smyrill came upon a hare which he chased with delight and all but caught, returning afterwards to pant at Olav's side and to walk along with him for a few minutes.

Now they seemed the only living things in this wide northern world. Men and ship had dropped alike below the horizon. Olav and Smyrill had no companions but the broad-faced sun.

Then, over the rise of one of the low ridges in front of them, a creature appeared. It was a wolf, unusually large and pale-coated. It did not run at seeing them, but stood watching for some time. Olav had never seen such a wolf—the eyes especially seemed somehow different from those of the wolves he had met with before. But before he could make out where the difference lay, the animal raised its muzzle, gave one long howl, and loped slowly away. Smyrill, who had been standing at the boy's side, growling deep in his throat, suddenly leaped after it. Olav called and shouted to him to come back, but for the first time, Smyrill paid no attention to him. It was as though he could not even hear his voice.

The wolf turned its head and quickened its pace, though it showed no sign of fear. If it stood a little less high in the shoulder than the dog, it was heavier and had not been staled by a sea voyage. Savagery at grips with courage, they would be well matched if they met.

Too well matched, Olav thought. He had no desire to have Smyrill torn half to pieces even if he killed the wolf. So he went after them, still shouting to Smyrill to come back, even when the two had disappeared from sight.

On the top of a rise he saw them again, far in the distance. The wolf had stopped and stood waiting, but Olav was relieved and yet astonished to see that Smyrill had also stopped about twenty feet away from his quarry. When the wolf trotted off again, Smyrill followed. When the wolf stopped, Smyrill stopped.

Olav cupped his hands about his mouth and shouted, but Smyrill did not turn his head. Before he could shout again, both had moved out of sight. The boy ran on. He was a good runner, but after an hour of the fast pace over uneven ground, he was winded and dropped to a walk. Another low swale of ground lay ahead of him, and climbing it wearily, he saw first the top of the low rise of land opposite, over which he thought he caught a glimpse of the wolf, still followed by the dog, disappearing again from view.

Olav was very tired now, but he could not give up the chase. Smyrill might be wounded and needing his help. He hurried over the top of the rise and saw the shallow plain at his feet.

But the plain was alive—a river of tossing horns and brown backs and cream-colored maned necks was passing down along it from the north. He could see the leaders, whose hoofs at this minute must be crushing out the faint recent tracks of wolf and dog alike. But to the north as far as he could look, the line of reindeer extended for at least four miles. They were traveling twelve or fifteen abreast, pausing to graze as they moved. Their horns looked like a great thicket of branches and from the line of their march rose a con-

tinual click of ankle bones and an occasional grunt as
a cow called to her calf.

Olav had never seen so many animals together. Air
and sea here in this manless region had for the most
part seemed thick with life, but now he saw that the
land could rival them. As he walked toward them, a
little bewildered by their presence, and not quite sure
how he was to pass through such a torrent of creatures,
a very faint mist began to rise from the lower land, and
the reindeer, which a short time ago had appeared so
clear, seemed now to be actually wading in another
river which rose from their knees to their shoulders and
at last reached the highest tips of their horns.

Olav, approaching them, himself entered into the
mist, which cooled and whitened the sunlight. The reindeer were very near now, pale spectral creatures which
paid no attention to him, but walked on in their column,
snatching at the grass and lichens as they walked. In
that pale light, weary and light-headed from hunger
and his long run, Olav himself felt almost disembodied.
Were these creatures moving in a mist, paying no attention to him, a dream? Or was he a dream? Or were they
and he all dreams on this endless plain?

Then he saw a woman walking between two reindeer, a hand on each of their necks. She was almost
invisible, for her white skin, the white woolen garment
she wore, her silver ornaments and her hair were all so
pale that they nearly faded into the mist through which
she moved. But her blue eyes were bright and Olav
could see them clearly. She was looking straight at him,
and she was smiling, and, with a little movement of
her head, she told him to come with her. The boy was
so amazed that even Smyrill was forgotten. Obeying

the gesture, he followed along to one side of the herd, looking at the woman who looked back at him, always smiling and always walking on.

Sometimes Olav lost sight of her altogether, and then he would run, panting and stumbling, until he saw her blue eyes again, but the reindeer seemed to go faster and faster. They were trotting now, and the woman ran between the two stags, looking at Olav over her shoulder, for he was losing ground. Hard as he tried to keep up, he was exhausted at last. She was frowning now. Her eyes looked angry. Then he stumbled and pitched forward, striking his head on the ground as he fell.

He must have lain unconscious for a long time. When he came to himself it was to feel a muzzle pushed down his neck.

He struggled up, ready to grapple with the wolf, but it was Smyrill, overjoyed to see him. There was no blood about the dog. He had been in no fight. He had no way of telling what had happened to him, but his eyes had a bewildered look as they stared into the bewildered brown eyes of his master.

Olav was glad to feel Smyrill's rough coat under his hands again, to feel bone and flesh and sinew, after the ghostly procession of the reindeer. The mist still lay in the lowest part of the valley like a long bodiless scarf. Perhaps woman and beasts had been only a dream of the mist. Rather unwillingly, Olav walked down to where they had been, but the plain showed clearly the signs of their multitudinous passing, where grasses and plants were flattened under their hoofs. The reindeer at least were no dream.

Once out of the valley and the mist, only weariness made the journey back to the ship difficult. Olav had come a long way. Now he retraced his steps through a blur of exhaustion, and Smyrill trailed at his heels.

Eirik met them about a mile from the shore. He had come to look for them.

"Toralde is dead," he told Olav. "A good man with his hands always. The only thing he could never do well was ride a horse. I have seen him thrown head over heels a dozen times. I shall miss talking with him of the old days. They will bury him tomorrow."

Olav nodded. "God rest his soul," he said.

Eirik looked at him with his glinting slanted eyes.

"What is wrong with you two? You look as though witches had been riding you."

When Olav told him the story, he looked grave.

"This wolf now, what kind of eyes had he?"

"Curious eyes. I don't know in just what way."

"Were they like a man's eyes?"

Olav thought. Then he said, "Perhaps."

"If they were a man's eyes, it was a runner-under-another-shape you saw. The only things such a man cannot change are his eyes. Whatever form he may take, his eyes remain the same."

"But what was his purpose?"

"Who can tell the purpose of such people? Perhaps to draw Smyrill off from you, so that he might attack you. Such people are usually bad, though not always. It may be that Smyrill kept between you, whatever the man tried. Or perhaps he was bringing you to the woman."

"I should have thought that in this land an elf woman would have had brown eyes."

"It was lucky that you were too tired to follow her any farther, or you would not have succeeded in getting back. The elves never let anyone go, once they have

taken them to their hills. Do not talk of these things to
the others. They would only mock at you and tell you
that you had fallen asleep and dreamed, or they would
have Sira Andres exorcise you against evil spirits. That
is a very wearisome occasion. I have gone through with
it several times, so I should know."

Olav had no desire to talk of the matter with anyone.
Indeed, he had no desire for anything but rest. He fell
asleep that night with Smyrill close beside him, too
tired even to eat; in the morning when he woke up to
a bright day of snapping wind and icebergs on the
horizon, the whole experience, even to him, seemed like
a dream.

Chapter *10*

The Skraelings

DAY AFTER DAY the Knarr sailed westward, but
she had been delayed too long. Ice was beginning to form. Olav, wakening in the night, could
hear its musical scrape and tinkle along the sides of the
the ship, and though it was as yet too weak to stop
their passage, it was slowly thickening into larger cakes
and the icebergs had reappeared. They had left the land
to the south of them but there seemed to be more far off
to the north. Once they passed along the shore of a
large island. Southward they saw nothing but water
with its drifting pans of thin ice.

"If we ever reach Karlsefni's Strawmfjord, we shall

be lucky," said Simon grimly. "I have no stomach for being crushed in the ice. This is not Vinland, sirs."

"What kind of place was Strawmfjord?" Paul asked.

"Good enough, until winter came. Then they had not enough provisions and nearly starved."

"God will take care of us," said Nicolas.

Orm was tired of hearing the phrase.

"You leave too much to God," he retorted. "It was your talk that led me to urge Paul so that the vessel was half-wrecked. God gave us brains to use them."

"Quarreling will improve nothing," Nicolas answered. "Perhaps we are meant to winter at Strawmfjord. From its name, I judge that the currents run high there."

"Pray we may get that far, Nicolas," said Orm, still out of humor, with both the King's Conscience and himself.

Good nature, in fact, was a rarer commodity on the Knarr than formerly. Everyone felt the tension of the gathering ice. The Swede, Johan Markusson, who on the voyage to Greenland and later at Vinland had been satisfied to grumble merely at details, now became a malcontent, and went about criticizing the leaders to anyone who would listen. Many men became taciturn. Simon, at the steering oar, snarled at anyone who spoke to him. There was quarreling over the draught games and loud words when one man jostled another.

Only Paul seemed entirely unaffected by the strain. He went about as calmly as ever, giving orders, talking to his companions, smacking his lips over his trencher. Now and then his laugh sounded, hearty and at ease.

"He is a real leader," Eirik admitted to Olav, "but Sigurd, your father, was more loved by his men. All this is nothing yet. We have only touched hunger with the tips of our fingers so far, and lost one man. Wait."

But this time the north, having stretched the cold shadow of its wings over them, withdrew once more. They had three days of southerly winds and the new ice drifted northward out of their course, and once more they sailed through the bright water. But the air was colder and the days no longer almost touched hands across the short barriers of the nights. The white whales still played at the surface of the sea, the walruses stared at them, the seals flipped off an occasional floating cake of ice into the water at their approach; but now when the birds passed overhead, their flight was always headed southward.

Then at last they saw land ahead, and after a day's coasting came to an island and a fiord backed by steeply rising land. There was grazing on the slopes and the current proved strong.

"You have followed a good course, Simon. Our people must have come here," Paul praised the pilot.

But when they put ashore they found nothing but some ruins of Skraeling huts of stone and sod, a few bones in a refuse heap and the marks of their fires. Everyone felt at a loss.

Orm offered a sensible explanation.

"There were Skraelings here when they arrived, and to avoid them, they sailed southward for Hóp without landing."

"That could well be, but I would be happier to have found some sign," Paul answered.

Still it seemed good to be sailing southward once more, this time with the land close by to the west. On the second day they came to a small bay where a stream emptied into the sea. Near its mouth were two Skraeling houses, so covered with turf that they were scarcely noticeable, but dogs ran to the beach, howling at first sight of the ship. A moment later six or seven men hurried down, and each getting into a small, sharp-ended boat, sped out to the Knarr, their double-bladed paddles flashing first to one side of them and then to another.

Olav and Eirik watched their approach from the rail.

"They look like the water spiders I used to see in the pools of our Hestnaes brook," Olav said. "Be still, Smyrill."

Paul had given orders not to bring the ship into the wind.

"The less we have to do with these people, the better. There seem to be few of them here, but they may have friends elsewhere. Sail on, Simon, we will leave them behind."

But he had counted without the lightness of the wind and the speed of the Skraelings' little boats. Instead of being left behind, the men rapidly grew closer, their dark flat faces widened still further with smiles. As they came within speaking distance, they broke into floods of unintelligible speech, and pulled out fine furs—white fox and ermine, and skins of the eider duck, and walrus tusks, waving them toward the Norwegians at the rail above them.

"Sail on, Simon," said Paul. "They will grow tired of this after a while, if we pay no attention to them."

"They are certainly like Vidar's wife, and dressed like her, too," said Benedikt.

Ulf suddenly struck the rail with his open hand.

"Look, Paul! That one over there; he's wearing a frieze coat!"

Now that their attention had been drawn to the clothing of the Skraelings, everyone saw something of interest.

"The boy has a red Norse stocking tied around his head."

"See, there, the last one! That thing through his nose is a copper spoon!"

"They have been trading with our people, surely," Paul declared. "Take her back to the anchorage, Simon. We must question them before going on farther."

When the Knarr rode at anchor, Paul would not allow the Skraelings to come near her.

"Push them off with oars," he said to his men. "I was told in Greenland that sometimes, under pretense of trade, they will come up to a ship and bore holes in her side close to the water line, so that she goes down in the first high seas. Orm, I leave you in charge. Station the men along all the rail and, whatever happens, see to it that no one comes nearer than the length of an oar. I will take one boat and go ashore to talk with these people. Ten of us should be enough, but be prepared to send in another boat if you see any disturbance. There seem to be five women and a few children on the beach, and there are six men and a half-grown boy in the boats. The men who go with me should wear their swords and each carry a light ax in his belt."

Everyone wanted to go ashore, but Paul smiled and silenced them with a motion.

"Nicolas goes," he said, "and Benedikt if he wishes, and, Johan Markusson, perhaps you will be in a better humor if you come. Eirik, they seem to be cousins of yours, you may make yourself understood better than the rest of us can. That means Olav, too, of course, but leave Smyrill or he will be torn to pieces by their dogs. Thorvald, Haakon, and Gunnulf, and Edvin over there by the mast—with me that makes ten—get your weapons and we'll be off."

"Can we bring something with us to trade?" asked Gunnulf.

Paul nodded. "But take no time in getting ready. Anything at hand."

As they rowed off, he called back to Orm. "Count them. They're following us. Make sure that one doesn't stay or come back."

"I will make sure."

"If we should stay until after dark, keep torches burning at bow and stern and along each side."

"None of them shall come near."

The Skraeling boats were at the beach before the Norwegians could land. Followed by their women, the men crowded about the newcomers, smiling and nodding at them, talking and making signs.

"Do not begin to trade yet," Paul ordered his followers. "I must ask them first about the Greenlanders. Eirik, come beside me. See how pleased they are at sight of you! They must think you are one of their own people who has somehow lost his tongue."

There followed an hour of talk in sign language, at first very much at cross-purposes, but as time drew on, the meanings became clearer to both groups. The leader among the Skraelings, who seemed to go by the name of Apiak, was an elderly man with a sly, sardonic face, a little taller and heavier than the others. It was he who wore the frieze coat, and for some time he kept trying to trade, looking most often at the fine ax in Paul's belt and his sword with its ivory hilt shaped like a horse's head.

But at last he saw that there would be no trade until the stranger's questions were answered. Making a face at which the other Skraelings laughed, he settled down in earnest to the task of understanding and making himself understood.

His coat, the spoon, the hood one of the women was wearing, yes, these things had come from just such people as these before him. He picked up a handful of skins and pretended to hand them to Olav and to take his cloak in return. Trade—they had had their things in trade. There were many, many of the strangers. He looked at the Knarr at anchor and shook his head. Then he made a pile of thirty or forty pebbles, sucked in his lips and nodded. So, so many had there been. Many, many boats. And people? He tapped a man and spread his arms wide; he tapped a woman and spread his arms less wide, and then, calling a child, showed that there had been more children than women.

Eirik, his slant eyes dancing, picked a late flower. He held it upright and whistled like the wind. With his hand he made motions of falling snow. The flower drooped. He covered it with his free hand. Then he pointed to the sun. He flapped his arms while the women giggled and buried their faces in their shoulders to hide their amusement. He whistled like a singing bird; the flower revived. It stood upright. Then came the pantomime of cold wind and ice. The flower drooped.

Apiak reached over and took the flower. He understood. Quickly he went through Eirik's pantomime. Eight times he raised the flower. The strangers had been here eight years ago. Then, grinning, not waiting for the next question, he pointed southward down the coast. He pulled at imaginary ropes and hoisted imaginary sails. Then, holding his skin coat out from his sides, he took a few steps toward the south, leaning back like a sail filled with the wind, while his people roared with

laughter. Suddenly Apiak gave an astonishingly realistic
moo followed by a series of bleats, until even the Norsemen laughed aloud. The man was a natural mimic.
Looking at him, they had seen the fleet sailing away,
and now they heard the cattle and sheep on the decks.

There could be no doubt but that they had come upon
a real and explicit trace of those they sought. Paul
looked well satisfied.

"Now trade, friends, to your hearts' content. Anything but weapons. Do not let them have so much as
a trencher knife."

Johan Markusson was unwise enough to grumble at
this, having brought several knives ashore in his cloak,
but Paul swung on him.

"The man who trades so much as one knife, stays
here when we sail, and sees how he likes the feel of it
between his ribs."

Olav had little he could spare besides his second-best
red cloak. It was threadbare now and torn, but the
Skraelings found no fault with it. He exchanged it for
twenty ermine skins with which Ingrid might some day
trim her own cloak if all went well. For the brooch which
had pinned it, he bought three white foxskins for his
mother, wonderfully thick and soft. But with cloaks
and pins the Skraelings were not really satisfied. Again
and again they showed the Scandinavians a little knife
which the Greenlanders had let them have eight years
before. It was such a little knife, but the man who
owned it treated it as if the finest of treasures. They
coaxed like children; they piled up all their furs, willing
to give everything for an ax, a sword. They offered a
woman, too. Apiak was particularly insistent, but it
was Paul's weapons which he wanted. He came close
to them, eyeing them with obvious greed, touching

them with his small, finely shaped hand, until Paul
motioned to him to keep farther away.

Only after a long time did the Skraelings give over
their attempt to buy weapons. It was late in the afternoon and everyone felt the exhilaration of bargaining.
Such furs and eiderdown socks and sealskin boots as
the Norwegians had bought, and such strange, bright
and glittering finery as the savages were putting care-
fully away in their houses! Even Apiak, who for a while
had seemed very much out of humor, was now smiling.
Olav had gone a little to one side, his trading being
quickly over. A little boy near him was playing with a
puppy. The child could not have been more than two
or three years old, round-faced as a doll, and breeched
and booted and coated like one of the men. Near by,
two or three dogs were nosing and rooting under some
stones and turf, covered by a sled at one side of one of
the houses. The rest of the people were at some distance,
still intent on the last buying and selling.

One of the dogs must have succeeded in getting at a
piece of whaleskin buried in a storage hole, for he backed
away with the thing, growling menacingly as he tried
to get clear of his companions. But with a roar, three
dogs leaped at him and the booty. Rolling over and
over, fighting savagely, growling and clawing, the four
dogs bore down on the little boy, who was too young to
get quickly up from where he sat with the puppy on
his lap.

But Olav sprang from his idle watching and caught
up the child and puppy together and just got out of the
path of the furious beasts with his new charges in his
arms. The uproar had drawn the attention of the Skraelings, and while a couple of men seized clubs and ran
to beat the dogs apart, a young woman came up and

took the little boy, looking at Olav very gratefully. In spite of the tattooing on her cheeks and chin, she had a pretty, gentle face and he smiled at her and praised the child as well as he could. She seemed to understand, and to thank him once more, before she went to join the other women, who were returning to the houses.

Apiak now came forward and invited the Scandinavians to eat with them. Paul did not agree to this at once, yet in the end accepted the invitation, partly hoping to learn something about their habits in eating which might be useful to know. He let seven of the men go into the larger hut, while he and Olav and Eirik followed Apiak and his two sons into the other house, where his daughters-in-law were already holding whale blubber over a stone lamp to heat it. One of the women looked up from her work and Olav saw that it was the mother of the little boy, and was surprised that she did not smile at him now, as she had before.

No one ever quite knew what strange food they were given to eat that night, but one thing was certain. The meat was nearly raw, and it was good. With it they ate sweet grass roots. Paul watched everything that Apiak did with great care and never ate until his hosts had eaten of the same meat, and Olav and Eirik followed his example in all they did. The feasting was lengthened out by Apiak's entertainment. He showed them his bone-tipped harpoons, with their detachable shafts of narwhal tusk, and their long walrus-hide thongs. He showed them a weapon made from half a dozen ivory balls fastened together by thongs. Whirl that at a bird, he made them understand, and the thongs wrapped themselves about its wings and it was yours. Knives of stone and bone were next brought out, but without so much as a glance this time at Paul's weapons. The

Norwegians found all these things ingeniously made and of great interest. They passed them from hand to hand in the faint light of the oil lamp, for there were no windows in the house and the daylight had died away from the tunnel which led to a door so low that a person must enter through it on his hands and knees. Sometimes the sons of Apiak said something, or brought something to show, but the women sat back in the shadows, one with the little boy in her arms, watching and listening, but silent.

Now there was something Apiak wanted to show them. He looked into a box made of whalebone, but it was not there. Next he looked on a shelf above the bed platform covered with skins on which Paul and Olav sat. But still he did not find it. He asked a son, who in turn gave a negative grunt.

"Very well, then, I will go get it," Apiak said, and so well did his body and face interpret his meaning, that the Norsemen almost understood the words. No one paid much attention as he crawled out of the room. It was only by chance that Olav happened to glance at the young woman with the child.

Her expression had changed. There was a warning in her eyes and almost imperceptibly she shook her head, and then bent down again to look at the sleeping boy in her lap.

Olav sat where he was for a moment, wondering if the woman's warning were something he had only imagined coming to him from the shadows beyond the yellow light of the stone lamp. But there had been danger in that look.

He rose from the sleeping platform, where he was sitting with Paul, and said casually, "I'll be back in a

minute. I want to ask Apiak something." Like all his
race, he could not bear to be laughed at, and he had
no wish to have Paul think him overcautious. Eirik,
sitting by the door, looked at him sharply as he stooped
on his hands and knees to go out. He had to crawl five
or six feet in that position. The skin curtain at the end
of the passage, which had been left open when they
went in, had been lowered. There was nothing strange
about this, as it was now night and colder, and Apiak
would naturally close the opening in going out. But
Olav waited a moment before he raised it in order to
take his ax from his belt.

As he paused, he heard Eirik's voice behind him in
the room, speaking with a sort of sinister playfulness.

"No, you don't, my sealskinned friend! Two are
enough outside at a time. You return where you were,"
and there was a sound of something like a scuffle.

"God be praised," Olav thought, "I shall have no
one at my back," and he cautiously lifted the curtain.
He had a choice between crouching there at the entrance, partly sheltered, while he looked about for
possible danger, or of going out directly and letting
the curtain fall behind him, risking a sudden attack
from the darkness before his eyes had become accustomed to the change of light. He chose the latter, not
daring to give his presence away by letting the narrow
glow from inside the house rest for more time than could
be helped before the doorway.

Once clear of the door, he rose silently to his feet and
stepped into the shadows of a small building used as
a storehouse for furs or food. He neither saw Apiak nor
heard him, but a dog came toward him, growled a
little and then went back to its fellows. Although the
sun had gone down and the sky was banded with

clouds, it was not really dark. The northern lights were leaping and tossing their colored spears along the horizon, and he could see the slope of the house he had just left outlined dark against them.

In the other direction the light was yellow-red. The torches which Orm had ordered lighted on the Knarr flared and burned above their reflections in the sea, and between the living flame of fire and the corpse flames to the north, a few stars, escaping the clouds, shone like white sparks.

Olav, pressed there against the rough stones of the shed, had no time to think of beauty. To him the lights were both friends and foes, for if they might help him to see Apiak, they also might lead Apiak to him. From Eirik he had years ago learned the art of immobility. He could be motionless for a long time and now he sent out his senses hunting for Apiak. Nostrils, eyes and ears explored the darkness, and the nostrils were the first to make a report.

Faintly the heavy smell of grease and dirt that marked the Skraelings came to him down what little wind there was, stirring past the house. Next, ears reported a soft scraping sound, as though something were dragging over sod, and last the straining eyes saw a darkness edge itself up along the darkness of the rounded roof of the hut, held low to that greater darkness, but still visible against the pulsing light behind.

While Olav shifted the ax in his hand to a balanced grip, he saw the figure cautiously lift the small skin which covered the smoke vent and glance down into the room where almost directly below Paul sat on the sleeping platform. For a moment the dark face was strangely lighted up, more like a skull's than a man's.

Apparently satisfied by what it had seen, the figure

LAND
WITH-
OUT
A
NAME

greenLand

iceLand

ARCTIC CIRCLE

EASTERN SETTLEMENT

WESTERN SETTLEMENT

helluLand

Ocean

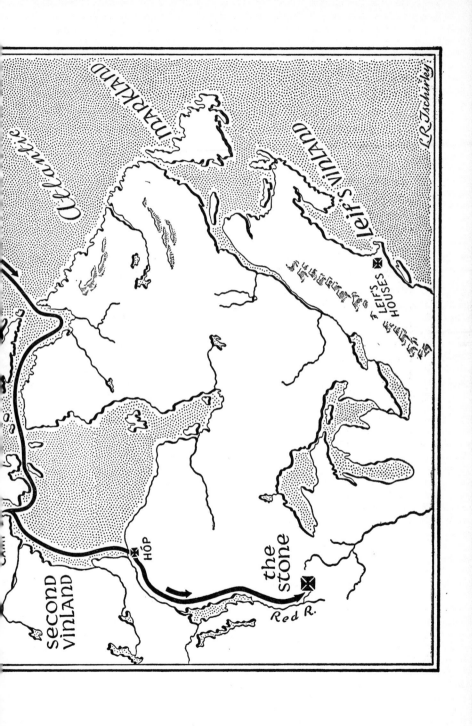

L R Tschirley

Atlantic

MARKLAND

Leif's Vinland

LEIF'S HOUSES

HÓP

the stone

Red R.

SECOND VINLAND

quickly put back the skin and rose to its feet; now Olav saw that there was a great harpoon in the man's hand, such as hunters use in hunting walruses. It was time to act. Olav sprang forward in silence and ran for the building, leaping onto the roof of the entrance and from there up the low sloping grass-grown roof of the house. The Skraeling was so intent upon his kill that for a moment he did not hear the boy's approach. Then suddenly he became aware, and swung to meet it, but too late by a fraction of time. Before he could change his grip on the handle of the harpoon and bring it up to face this unexpected attack, Olav had raised his ax and struck down, down twice, first on the man's left arm flung up to protect his head, and the second time with all his strength on the head itself.

Apiak gave a grunt and fell, and Olav, wrenching free the ax, knew that there was no need for a third blow. He heard a sound at the entrance and made out the figure of Paul getting to his feet with drawn sword.

"What has happened?" Paul asked in a low voice.

"I have just killed Apiak. He was going to harpoon you through the smoke vent."

Eirik backed out through the tunnel, his ax in his mouth.

"Stay here and see that no one else comes out of the house," Paul said to him, "while we go to call the others."

There were seven men in the larger Skraeling dwelling and at Paul's orders they came out, guarding their rear from possible attack.

"Pile the doorway with stones or anything you can find," Paul ordered. "We don't want them swarming out like hornets until we are gone."

Actually not a sound came from either house as the

Scandinavians sweated and strained at the stones under the effortless shifting play of the northern lights.

"That will hold our foxes in their burrows for a while," said Paul at last. "Now down to the boat, friends, and let us be off."

He stood by the gunwale of the boat and counted the men as they got in.

"Where is that boy?" he shouted. "Eirik, where is he?"

But Olav ran up just then, having changed his ax for his sword.

"I slit their skin boats," he said as he clambered in, "and a larger undecked boat, too, that I found beyond the others."

"Good boy," said Paul, pushing off, the last man to get in. "They won't soon forget our visit." But on board the Knarr, telling Orm of what had occurred, as the anchor was pulled up and the sail hoisted for a run farther off the dangerous shore, Paul said, "I am sorry that blood was shed."

Eirik was standing near by.

"Would you rather it had been your own?" he asked, with a touch of anger.

"I said only that I was sorry that blood had been shed."

"And I say only that you have given small thanks to Olav for saving your life."

Paul's face, in the light of the torch by which he stood, turned dark with mantling blood and he frowned at Eirik.

"I need no Lapp to give me lessons. The boy showed good sense and did his duty. Anyone here would have done the same."

Orm hastened to change the subject.

"It is lucky that most of you left the furs for which you had traded in the boat, so that they at least are not lost by this misadventure. From what you say, the man must have been beside himself with greed for your weapons."

"No doubt," said Paul, but he was in an ill humor and would talk no more that night.

In the morning, as they sailed southward for Hóp, he did come to where Olav sat on the deck playing chess with Benedikt. His thick shadow lay across Olav's hand on the board.

"No, don't stop your game," he said stiffly. "I only wished to say that you behaved well last night."

Olav thanked him, and, getting to his feet, waited.

Would Paul, having made a start, go on? Would he say that Olav had acted with courage? But to say such a thing was to acknowledge himself in the wrong. When he should do that, he must admit that here was no coward's son, and that he, Paul Knutson, had miscalled his dead comrade at arms. He must admit that God had judged between them, and that he had been but a false friend. The old betrothal to Ingrid must be reacknowledged. No, Paul was not ready for so much. He looked older and for the first time tired, as he repeated wearily, "You behaved very well last night," was silent, sighed, and turned away.

Benedikt said under his breath, "The old lion smarts at being beholden to you."

"It is but natural," said Olav, sitting cross-legged again. "Your move, Benedikt."

The ship sailed on. Again they were in skim ice, but now even Simon believed that they would reach Hóp in time, and the men could talk of little else but of the welcome they would receive.

"They have been there eight years," Gunnulf declared. "My cousin, Haftor, should have a good farmstead by now. Perhaps Margret and I will stay on there instead of returning to the Western Settlement. We will see when we know better what Hóp is like."

Hóp! The Place of the Landlocked Waters! Sira Andres said that the name reminded him of the psalms of King David, "Thou leadest me beside the still waters," and as he talked, Olav thought of many sheep, feeding so close to a lake that their reflections grazed upside down at their feet. Ingrid walked among them, wearing a white cloak edged with ermine. Her eyes were as blue as the elf woman's had been in the Reindeer Valley. So Olav dreamed, and knew that he was dreaming.

But even when wide awake he thought of Hóp as of the place where their mission would at last come to an end in prayer and rejoicing.

Paul had offered his trencher dagger with its hilt of carved amber to the man who first saw Hóp. Even without the offer of a reward, all eyes continually strained ahead for the first glimpse of the new settlement which they were so sure lay to the south. One day they passed an empty fishing hut on a bay.

"Norse work!" everyone cried, crowding the rail. "See! No Skraeling builds so." It was not the fishing season, and there was no boat on the shore, so they did not stop to examine the building, being anxious to go on. Better to meet the builder than his work, thought they, but the hut made one more proof that they were indeed coming near their mark.

It was at dawn of a cold morning, when the sun, swinging unwillingly up into the sky, looked white with haze, and a thin fog hung between the sea and the shore, that Ulf, the outlaw, who had the keenest eyes on the ship, suddenly shouted: "Hóp lies ahead!"

Everyone ran forward to share the vision. Faintly they could make out a bar of sand, and behind it at some distance buildings, one or two of them relatively large, but in the light fog they could not be certain of the details.

"See, there are farmsteads scattered along the valley!" Gunnulf told anyone who would listen. "In one of them I shall find Margret."

"Let us sing a hymn of thanksgiving to God, who has led us here in safety!" Nicolas was transfigured with delight. "Sira Andres, lead us, so that they on shore may first be aware of our coming by the holy sound."

The men's voices all rose together in a Latin hymn filled with solemn triumph as they approached toward shore.

Simon, seeing that the water here was very shallow, sent two men forward with weighted lines to warn him when the Knarr must be anchored. They sang as they drew in the lines and swung them out again. Even Simon sang at the steering oar, and the harsh lines of Johan Markusson's face smoothed out their discontent, and even Ulf's eyes lost their wild-hawk look, and Paul's weariness was laid aside like an old coat.

When the hymn had come to an end, they listened, half-hoping to hear its noble sound echoed from the shore. When they heard nothing, they were not discouraged.

"Perhaps we are farther off than we realize," Orm said; "distances in this land are tricky."

"It is time to anchor, the water is very shoal," Simon declared. "As it is, the Knarr may be left on the flats at low tide."

But all knew that even were this to be true, the ship would be no worse for the experience. They lowered the two boats on deck beside the stern boat, and all took their places, save for a couple of men who unwillingly enough stayed aboard at Paul's orders.

As they began to row, the singing broke out again. The mist was clearing. It would be a beautiful day.

Eirik, who shared a rowing bench with Olav, said in a low voice under the singing, "Just the same, I do not like the feel of this place."

But the music closed over his words and Olav scarcely heard him.

Chapter 11

Winter at Hóp

THERE were no people to meet the boats when they grated up the shore. There was no smoke falling off from the roofs of the buildings which stood beyond where the river widened almost to a lake behind the sandbars. No human voices, no sound of cattle or sheep rose beyond those still waters, only the cawing of some crows rising up from the fields, late to start on their pilgrimage to the south. When Olav was a little boy at Hestnaes, his mother's woman, Ingeborg, used to tell him that the birds, too, had a shrine somewhere far to the south, raised in honor of the white dove into which the spirit of God had entered. All summer

they sang in Norway and worked to raise their families
and then, like good people, their duties done, they
journeyed southward to their shrine.

"That is what the birds are talking about now, little
Olav. Soon they will fly away and we shall not see
them until next year. They learn all their pretty songs
to sing before the statue of Our Lady and the little
Jesus. When they come back, how well they sing! But
you will notice that as summer goes on, they sing less
well, and by the time the harvest has been reaped, they
have almost forgotten their songs. They have to go
south to learn them again. When you hear a bird sing,
he is praising God."

It was years since Olav had thought of the birds'
shrine. The parish priest had merely smiled and shaken
his head once when he had asked him about it. But
now, numb with disappointment, he remembered Ingeborg's tale and wondered if the birds of the Western
Islands also worshiped God.

Almost in silence, save for the prayers that Nicolas
and Sira Andres were saying in undertones, Paul led
the way toward the nearest buildings. There were two
or three houses near the lake, built close together with
their barns and byres and storehouses grouped about
them. They were all of stone except for one building,
whose western end had been made of timbers. It might
have been a church. Two church bells lay beside it on
the ground, but they had never been raised. The barns
had been used, but not for some time. Back of them
they found heaps of the bones and horned skulls of
cattle and there were rams' skulls and the skeletons
of sheep in the piles.

Orm said, "They have killed their beasts. This has a
bad look."

Near the building which they took to have been the church, there were graves, fifty or sixty of them, their small wooden crosses already tipped and staggering. Here the newcomers knelt, and Sira Andres led them in prayers for the dead. This graveyard in the empty wilderness seemed haunted by the exiled spirits of those who lay below the thin earth far from any sound of speech or human action.

"There was some extraordinary sickness among them, poor souls," Paul mused.

By the shore of the lake they found a dozen boats, turned upside down and covered over with boards and turf, but they already had begun to rot, here and there.

Paul had put off going into the houses until the end. Everyone shared his feeling of dread. Once again they had come to an empty shell of life, as they had at the Western Settlement, but this time they felt cheated and at a loss. Here their people had been, here built their farmsteads and pastured their animals. Everywhere were the signs of their presences and activities. But now they were gone like the fog.

Paul pulled the latch thong of the largest house and went in. Except for some work of rats, the place was still in order. The thin gut across the windows had not even been broken, and there were the ashes of a last fire in the fireplace in the center of the room.

Some attempt had been made to carve the bedsteads of the two built-in beds and the uprights of the high seats which stood between them, but the work was hasty and without assurance, as though the man who had done the carving had not felt that it was worth the trouble of doing. The benches were in their places along the walls and there were footstools near the fireplace. One or two white bear rugs had been left in the

next high tide they floated the Knarr through the shallow mouth of the lake. It took a prodigious amount of hauling and pushing with boats and oars, but was finally accomplished. Paul was everywhere, encouraging and praising, lending a hand with the hard rowing in the small boats, shouting to Simon on the deck. Before they got her across, they had to lighten her of the remaining cargo, but by nightfall the forty men were established in the two largest houses, somewhat hastily cleaned and with fires on the hearths.

But it was a ghostly life they lived in the ruins of other people. Leif's old houses in Vinland had not had this tragic air, for they had been built originally as a temporary winter camp and from time to time had been used as such. But these houses at Hóp had been built for a permanent colony. Here men had chosen the sites for their farmsteads on this slope of plain or that, and measured out the foundations of their dwellings. This country was open and suitable for pasture, but there were also black cockscombs of low spruce and larch woods patterning the land, where firewood could be got. Hopes must have risen high at first, but with the hopes there must from the beginning have been doubts as well. Only in the largest house had any carving been done, and that was half-hearted; the church bell had never been raised, and some of the buildings, begun perhaps toward the end, were unfinished. Karlsefni's earlier failure at Hóp must have shadowed all the undertaking.

Later on, when they had much leisure, Olav and Eirik thought that they found some of Karlsefni's old stonework incorporated in the new buildings, but they would never know for sure. The colonists had left Hóp in the spring of 1359, a year before Magnus Eirikson had talked with the Greenlanders, and Nicolas Byrgeson had roused the king's easily inflamed enthusiasm for a new crusade.

During the fall, while the men were busy hunting and cutting and hauling firewood, there was small talk of plans for the spring. But as the snows grew heavier and game became scarce and there was more and more loitering by the hearth, the muttering began.

"We have enough to report to the king. Why should we all lose our lives for a hammer or two on eating bowls? There are hammers in Norway, if Magnus searched long enough. Even Nicolas would have to admit that there are crosses on all the graves. This is our second winter away from home. It is time to return. These men are Christian enough for all purposes. Why should we follow their mad wanderings farther?"

Such talk could be heard any day whenever the leaders were out of earshot. Paul knew well enough what was being said and countered it by detailing his plans for pushing up the river in the small boats as soon as the ice was out. He took note, meanwhile, as to what men were in the center of the knots of malcontents. Johan Markusson, the Swede, and a young Norwegian named Halvard found themselves oftenest ordered into the woods or to the fishing, which was still being carried on through the ice, and complained bitterly that they were being treated with injustice.

Paul laughed when at last they rebelled at his order to go out woodcutting at the tail of a fall of snow.

"It is good for you fellows," he said. "Sitting about the fire makes you splenetic. The air brightens your cheeks and stills your tongues."

Under his glance they put on their heavy outer clothes and went, for Paul's good humor had an

element behind it which no one as yet was quite prepared
to face. It was not very cold; warmer perhaps than in
Norway. The winter went well enough, and the firewood never gave out, but more than once they sat
down to nothing but a bowl of thinnest broth made
from bones and hides. Yet actual starvation they did
not face. Although in the late winter some sickness
again appeared among them, no one died.

Slowly the long days lengthened, the snows began to
melt and the ice to bend and crackle in the lake. Then
suddenly the wind turned southerly. Water ran in a
thousand veined streamlets under the rotten snow and
over the bare grasslands, the first duck and geese returned, filling the air with their cries which often
sounded like the barking of dogs, and Ulf began to
sing at the top of his lungs as he mended his clothes on
the south doorstep.

"Soon we shall be off south," he said to Johan, who
came by lugging firewood. But his attempt to provoke
the Swede to an answer failed, for the man only looked
sullen and turned away.

For a few days Ulf and Benedikt, Gunnulf, Olav and
the rest of the young men spent hours in wrestling bouts
and races and in shooting and throwing spears at a
target. The grim settlement rang with their boisterous
play. Paul watched it, smiling.

"Eirik," he said. "Ulf thinks he is a champion wres-
tler. Go and teach him how we wrestled when we were
young," and the Lapp, grinning, stepped out to face
Ulf, like a gnome facing Baldur the Beautiful, and
threw him within two minutes. No one could beat him,
either, at the spear-throwing, but he was not so good
with the bow, and bad in the foot races. Olav won these

last. After a winter on land, he had regained his old swiftness and endurance, and though he did not win at the shooting of the arrows, which was Ulf's game above all, he came in second.

For a few days, until the river was free of ice, Paul let the young men rejoice in the spring. Then he called a meeting in the hall and said that the next morning they would begin preparations for going southward.

"I know there are some who think that we should give up the quest and go home," he said. "I myself was of that mind until we found the keel on Bird Island, but now I think it our duty to follow where the others have clearly led the way. If any man prefers to take one of the boats down by the water and sail for Greenland, I shall let him go." He looked directly at Johan and Halvard. "You two there, beyond Eirik. Are you for Greenland?"

"The boats are rotten," said Johan sullenly. "Give us one of the boats we brought on the Knarr and we will go."

"They are needed. What, Swede, can't you even mend a boat? Well, now, who goes to Greenland?"

There were mutters, but no one spoke up. They remembered the long voyage, the danger, the naked islands and reefs, the ice. No one wished to face them in a single leaky boat without a proper leader or Simon's wisdom at the steering oar.

"No one speaks? You had words enough this winter, Halvard. Johan, you are now afraid, but then you were bold enough with your tongue. Come, come, my heroes, why should you turn away from a summer voyage?"

The men reddened with anger, but were silent.

"No one for Greenland, then," said Paul at last.

"With Simon here, we make forty men. He takes the place of Toralde, God give him good rest. Thirty men will go south with me, and ten remain here. Orm, it is fitting that you should remain in charge of the Knarr and our stores at Hóp."

Orm said quietly, "I will do what you say, Paul."

"Simon, too, to keep the Knarr in repair."

Simon nodded. It had always been assumed that his place was with the ship.

Then Paul named one of the troublemakers, the young man Halvard. "But Johan shall go with us. Two of you together is one too many." Halvard looked relieved at staying. Paul named three more Swedes, solid trustworthy men, and Nicolas, but Nicolas protested excitedly.

"You are not strong enough for such a venture," Paul explained. "So far, we have slept soft and eaten well, if sometimes sparingly. But what lies ahead is a different story. Every man who goes will have to work at the oars from before dawn until darkness falls. We will sleep on wet ground and eat as we may. You have a great heart, Nicolas, but this is beyond you."

"When I can go no farther, I will die, Paul, but you must not turn me back from serving God in the manner that was given to me to do." Paul yielded.

Fat, meat-loving Sira Andres proved no easier to leave behind.

"I need to do penance for my gluttony," he said, half in jest, half in earnest. "No, Paul, I shall expect no favors, but shall work beside you, even if I cannot run like Olav and the others."

"Then Eirik and the boy will stay."

Olav jumped to his feet.

"Why do you always call me 'boy,' Paul Knutson?"

he demanded, flushing. "Have I not done a man's share
up to this time? Am I not now as tall as you are? I will
not be left behind!"

"I thought you would prefer not to go with me."

"If I had preferred that, I should still be with Magnus
Eirikson at Bergen. Would you evade God's judgment
on our case?"

Paul checked some angry answer, and said simply,
"I have little name for evasions. Come if you will, you
and your Lapp and your dog. Before we are through,
Smyrill may have a chance to show if he is good at
tracing."

The next two men he named were content enough to
stay at Hóp.

When the three boats were equipped and ready to
start several days later, Paul gave Orm his final instruc-
tions before them all.

"You are in full command here for the king, Orm.
Keep a watchful eye out for Skraelings and see that
no harm comes to the Knarr. Lay in all the smoked fish
and meat that you can and if there are berries on these
bushes, dry them—you will need to plan for all of us
for next winter in case we return while the river is still
open. If we do not return then, you can be sure that
we have died or that we have followed the Greenlanders
eastward to Vinland. When the ice goes out in the
spring, try to join us at Leif's Houses. If you have lost
men, you may have to stop at Greenland for more, but
come as soon as you can. If we have not reached Leif's
Houses by the end of next summer, you may give us
up, and leave for Norway as soon as you judge best."

Orm said: "We understand your orders, Paul. Go,
and God be with you."

"God be with you, too," said Paul, embracing him.

All those who were to enter in upon the unknown, the nameless wilderness, and the handful who were to remain in the deserted settlement, walked down together to where the three boats lay, drawn up on the shore of the wide estuary.

Paul had spoken truly, when he said that the hardships they had undergone up to this time were merely shadows of those they would now know.

Long before dawn each day he was awake.

"Up, men, up!" came his shout, and Nicolas' high voice would join him. "Up! No more sleeping. Up!"

No matter how exhausted Nicolas had been the night before, unable to eat, ghastly as a walking spirit, crawling off, broken, to lay his wolfskin rug in some shelter, by morning his strength had somehow revived, and he was shouting with Paul, and shaking the shoulders of the late sleepers, making the same little jokes about their love of ease. Fat Sira Andres sweated at the oars with the best, and sang hymns valiantly as they struggled against the strong current of the river. He had a burly strength under his fat that no one had rightly suspected. Olav, though his hands were blistered, stood the strain well enough, and Eirik from the first showed no signs of fatigue. Sitting beside Olav at the oars, he would talk about the Greenlanders who must have made this journey three springs earlier.

"I wonder, now, if the women took a hand at rowing?" he would say out of a long silence. Or again, "They needed many fewer boats, what with the cattle gone and the people they had lost. But we found no goats' skulls. Were the goats still with them?"

Another time, when they found the child's grave at a turn of the river, he talked about the children. "What

a life for little ones!" he pondered. "And yet they have
known nothing but this land at the ends of the earth.
To them it must seem familiar—as Norway to you.
They must even be accustomed to seeing no one but
their relatives. Probably they can scarcely believe that
there are any other people in the world."

An average day saw them eating dried meat in the
darkness as they rolled up their sleeping rugs and
pushed out the boats into the river as the first light
paled the sky. After five hours of rowing, they drew up
to the shore and ate again and once more at noon or a
little later. Only when darkness fell did they light fires
and eat hot food. Every day was a little longer than
the one before it, but they grew sparer and harder with
the days. Their bleeding palms healed, their arms and
backs strengthened. Now jesting became natural, not
an effort of will. Sometimes the river ran quietly, sometimes swiftly. Sometimes they jumped out into ice-cold
shallows to drag the boats over rapids; very often they
went ashore and followed old carries hacked through
the scrub bushes that lined the river, past some falls
or rapids too deep for wading, rolling their boats on
rollers, or occasionally carrying them. But they were
very heavy.

Every four or five days they had to camp while the
hunters went in search of fresh meat. Paul usually
stayed with the boats and Nicolas always, resting his
weak body, impatiently nursing it while he could, so
that he might the better drive it on again next day.

The weather was shifting from spring to summer, and
they had much rain and several times sleet. The river
seemed to delight in plaguing them with boulders and
waterfalls, but they had two causes of satisfaction:
game was plentiful, and they saw almost daily the

evidence of the Greenlanders ahead of them. At the
carries they could see where their predecessors had cut
down the stunted trees; sometimes they found the
stains of old campfires, and once near one of these Ulf,
the keen-eyed, picked up a fire steel, shaped like a
serpent with head and tail twisted back.

"They cannot have traveled as fast as we have come,"
said Eirik. "There are many more of them and they
have the weak ones with them—and goats. See what I
have found? Here is a skull that can only be a goat's.
If they had milk, they had better meals than we have.
But I suppose the milk was only enough for the children."

"We do well enough," replied Olav. Baked with the
sun, thinned with hard work, he felt merry. Each day
he proved his strength and manhood against the wiles
of the river. Each day he saw country which he had
never seen before, and he loved hunting with Eirik
and Smyrill, who proved to have a wonderful nose for
picking up even a cold scent, and perfect fearlessness
in a attack. But usually Olav called him back when
they had come up with the quarry. Often the river
went through barren lands, but sometimes again they
entered for a while into a stretch of small trees. They
made good time. Here, as Paul said, they were not
delayed by fogs or head winds. Their own arms and
backs were enough for their voyage, fought endlessly
against the swift wide current, "oar wind" he called it,
jesting.

The weather grew more settled, and the air warmer.
Their chief difficulty was with stinging insects, and
they made smoky fires at night to drive them off. Eirik
found a bitter herb whose odor the flies did not like
and they rubbed its juice on their hands and faces. But

as time went on they grew accustomed to the stings and felt them less.

The most surprising thing about the journey was that without exception, they all enjoyed it. Even Johan Markusson had stopped grumbling. In lifting a boat, he and Sira Andres did better than anyone else.

After some weeks they came to a great lake out of which the river flowed. Here they set up the masts and sails they had brought with them and for five days sailed, both by sunlight and by moonlight, for the most part, out of sight of land, while the men lolled in their places. The lake was the largest they had ever seen, but everything in this land seemed to be very large. There was an animal that they had caught glimpses of, and had once killed, a huge deer with thick shovel-shaped horns and long legs and a tassel of hair halfway down its neck. No creature in Norway or Greenland for that matter could compare with it in size and a kind of ugly dignity. Almost every night they could hear wolves howling and sometimes they came very close to the camp. Smyrill would bristle and stand growling and glaring, but Olav never let him leave the sheltering glow of the campfire to battle with these waiting shadows.

At the head of the lake they found the mouth of a river. Its waters were stained by the earth through which it had run and they called it the Red River.

"I do not like this," said Eirik. "It looks like blood."

But they had no choice. The river came from the south and up it they went, mostly through a level land of plains. Now and then the banks were worn down into deep gullies with a wide trail at the bottom, as though for ages cattle had used them when coming to drink. But whose cattle these could be—if they *were*

cattle—they could not guess. There were often hawks
circling overhead and the sky was very hot and wide
and blue. When Olav climbed the bank at noon he
could look in every direction as far as the eye could
see over a rolling ocean of grass and flowers, and catch
no sight of tree or hill or sign of life, unless a bird sprang
up from underfoot or a long-legged hare with enormous
ears and a white tail loped off at his approach.

Paul studied the sun.

"It seems to me that by now we should be turning
eastward for Vinland," he remarked to Nicolas. "This
is a very great island. We will go too far if we are not
careful."

The Greenlanders must have had the same idea on
their earlier journey, for the very next day when Paul's
party reached a fork coming into the Red River from
the east, they found a broken oar driven into the bank
fifty feet up the new stream as a sign.

"And yet," said Benedikt that night, talking of the
matter at the campfire, "they could not well have
expected anyone to follow them."

"No," agreed Ulf, "but here, where we are lost to all
human knowledge, where only the hawk and the wolf
know our course, we must pretend that what we do
has a human meaning, that others of our kind will know
and care."

"Our position is comfortable compared to theirs,"
said Sira Andres. "We know that they are ahead; they
do not guess that we are behind. So far as they know,
their nearest neighbors are at the Eastern Settlement in
Greenland—in another world."

Eirik spoke up from where he sat, mending a worn
shoe.

"Oh, Sira Andres, they and we have nearer neigh-

bors. This land is not empty. No, I feel people here.
We shall find out, all in good time."

It was the very next day that his words were proved
true. At a bend of the stream, so that the defenders
were partially protected on three sides by the river
itself, they came upon earthworks apparently dug in
haste.

"Whoever is leading them knows how to pick out a
good point of defense," Paul said, giving the order to
pull in toward the shore. As they climbed to the earth
fort, no one spoke his fear, but everyone was relieved
to find no skeletons lying about on the turf within. The
defenders had apparently withstood some sharp, but
probably short attack, and had then gone on when the
enemy had dispersed. But they had suffered in the defense. In the middle of the ring of earth, one of the
Greenland boats had been left, turned upside down
with its sides piled up with dirt to protect what lay
buried beneath it, in a land which had no rocks. The
men, standing about it, did not need to count the
seventeen crosses burned into the wood to know that
here dead men and women had been buried.

"God rest their souls," said Sira Andres in a troubled
voice. "We can at least give them our prayers."

As they went back to the boats, Ulf exclaimed loudly,
"I am anxious to meet these Skraelings and see what
manner of men they are."

But they saw no sign of Skraelings, or of Greenlanders
either, as they rowed up this new, narrower river,
whose current was growing swifter.

The next day Paul announced that they must camp
and hunt.

"But keep your eyes in your heads," he warned. "Go
three or four together and look where you are going."

Ulf, Benedikt, Eirik, Olav and Smyrill started off in one group. Outlaw, courtier, Lapp, boy and dog, they had a liking for one another's company and often hunted together. Benedikt, who had seemed at court a creature of mere airs and graces, had a constitution of steel. He could match Ulf in any undertaking and never complained of hunger or exhaustion. As for Eirik, to all appearance he felt neither. Olav, though it was sometimes far from easy, held his own with the other three. Whoever else might come back empty-handed, it was never they.

Led by Eirik, they moved away from the river. To the eastward there were distant hills and the country was rolling. They walked in single file, not talking to one another. Smyrill had run off after one of the long-legged rabbits, but he always rejoined them as soon as Olav whistled him back.

As they came over a low upward curve of prairies, they saw two people and the carcass of some very large animal close at hand. One of the people looked up, saw them, ran off, swiftly and silently, disappearing among some stunted trees that unexpectedly grew near the spot. The other figure had been kneeling, fastening the strap of a heavy pack of meat across its forehead. Struggling to its feet, it threw off the load, and turned as though to run, then hesitated, and finally came slowly to meet the four men.

"Skraeling!" said Ulf very low. "Now you shall pay for the seventeen crosses!"

"Fool!" Eirik struck up his hand. "It is a woman. And see what she wears at her breast."

"Greetings, friends," said the Skraeling in good Norse, and then stood smiling at them with an air at once open and modest.

Chapter 12

The Cross

IF A BIRD had begun to sing in Latin, if a bear had knelt and made the sign of the cross, Olav could not have been more surprised. His dark eyes were wide with astonishment in his tanned face.

"Now we shall learn everything!" he exclaimed to Eirik, who alone among the four had kept his head enough to answer the woman's greeting.

Ulf now chimed in harshly, "Greetings, Skraeling woman!" Benedikt said, "Good day to you, pretty young maiden," and Olav, too, murmured a "God be with you."

"Where are the others?" Eirik asked, but the woman

only shook her head to that and all their other questions. Frantic at this sudden barrier, they surrounded her, asking about the Greenlanders, speaking more and more loudly as though by the very volume of their voices they could at last force their meanings into the woman's brain. But she shook her head to everything.

In the end she said very clearly "thank you," and then "good day," and turned up the palms of her hands, empty.

That was all of the Norse tongue that she knew.

But there she stood, a Skraeling more like the man whom Olav and Eirik had seen in Vinland than the round-faced people in the north. Benedikt had been right when he called her fair. She was tall enough, slim, with an oval face, regular dark features and lively eyes. Her dress was made of doeskin, and had a fringed skirt, and on her feet she had leggings and soft leather shoes, all trimmed fancifully with some bright-colored quills. Her hair was arranged in two braids and about her neck on a thong hung a large cross cut from copper. Whoever she was, wherever she came from, she had certainly met with the Greenlanders. Eventually her companion reappeared, a young man wearing only a breechclout, long leggings and leather shoes, with a necklace of bears' claws and copper armlets. He was as friendly as the young woman, but knew even less Norse than she.

While their attention was turned upon her companion, the woman drew out from a pouch at her belt two closed clamshells in which a few embers were still glowing, and with them she relighted a fire from some charred ends of old wood. Soon she had broiled some of the meat from the animal they had killed.

The four had never tasted better meat. They ate all

they could hold and Smyrill, who had long ago returned, had his share when they were through. The Skraelings smiled to see their enjoyment, and motioned them to tie up Smyrill to one of the near-by trees. Then taking a large wolf pelt and his bow and arrows under his arm, the man motioned for them to follow.

"Is it safe to go with this fellow?" Ulf demanded.

"Nothing is safe, friend," said Eirik, "but I smell no treachery here."

For an hour they followed their guide along the back of a series of low swales. Then they began to hear many sounds beyond them, a confusion of slow tramplings, of grass being torn up near the roots, of grunts and suddenly a distinct moo and a calf's bleating answer.

The Skraeling dropped to his hands and knees and with a cautioning look at the others, covered his head with the head of the wolf hide which hid his back and upper arms and legs and with his bow in one hand and his arrows in another, crawled over the rise. He made a strange-looking wolf to a close observer, but among the long grasses, he seemed wolfish enough to a passing glance.

The other four crawled after him and lay watching from the summit of the rise, screened by the prairie growth.

Olav had thought that the reindeer he had seen in Reindeer Valley were a great wonder, but their numbers were nothing to what he saw now. Where the reindeer had gone twelve or fifteen abreast, the herds of these great humped shaggy bulls and cows stretched away as far as he could see in every direction. They were feeding in tens and hundreds and thousands, black and lowering as thunderclouds, with their red calves about them. The nearest bulls paid no attention to the wolf which

appeared down wind from them, but two calves which
were butting heads, gave up their play and moved in
behind the buttresses of their mothers. On all the grown
animals blackbirds were perched, feeding on the insects
which hovered about their backs and rumps where the
hair grew thin. The massed curly hair covered the
creatures' heads and humped shoulders and hung in
bearded manes on their necks, but the rest of their
bodies looked more like those of tame cattle. They had
horns like cattle, too, plain and not very large, seen
among all those curls. With heads hung heavy and low,
they had a sleepy, sullen look, as they grazed or stood
lazily chewing their cuds in the noonday sunlight.

As for the despised wolf, it crept among them, actually going unnoticed past two or three of the older bulls
feeding at the edge of the herd. Then it drew in upon
itself and suddenly there came the sharp twang of the
bowstring and a yearling calf went down, struggled to
its feet, and went down once more, as the bowstring
twanged again and again. A young bull joined it on
the ground, and now the rest were moving away at
a trot which turned into a gallop. Heads down, short
tails in the air, they ran in a dark billowing mass, their
hoofs thundering heavily over the ground. It was not
a stampede, for a mile away they slowed down and soon
were feeding again, and the disturbed birds which had
followed their flight dropped down once more among
them, as dark as the great beasts on which they attended.

The Skraeling had thrown off the wolfskin he had
worn and had swiftly despatched the wounded animals.
Now he showed the others what parts of the meat to
take and how to make up their packs, and carried a
load himself as far back as his own camp by the trees,
which they now saw grew around a spring in damp

earth trampled by generations of these nameless animals. Here everything was nameless: the land, the river they traveled, these people with whom they had met, the huge beasts they had seen killed, the spring to which they had come. All, all alike were anonymous wonders, for which they had no familiar appellations. But the Skraelings at least took on the reality of names. Eirik pointed to the others and himself, repeating Ulf, Benedikt, Olav, Eirik, and the man and woman seemed to understand and said Ohenaw and Shakaka when in turn he pointed to them. The Scandinavians felt friendlier as soon as they could think of the strangers as Ohenaw and Shakaka. By every means in their power they tried to urge them to come back to the river with them, so that Paul might talk with them, but the Skraelings would not go in that direction, but pointed southwesterly and let it be understood that they must travel in that direction and quickly, having already delayed too long to help the strangers.

Was it possible that they would see the Greenlanders where they were going? But the four could not make their meaning clear, nor would the Skraelings delay any longer.

"Still," said Benedikt, "some message we must send," and he took a silver band from his arm and had Olav scratch on it with his dagger: "In the name of God, come to us at once." He gave it to the woman, Shakaka, putting it in her hand and making gestures as though she were giving it to some unseen person.

She giggled and seemed to understand, but did she? Still they could do no more, except that Eirik at the last moment gave Ohenaw a small dagger, in return for the help he had given them that day in hunting.

"There is no need to tell Paul of this," he said to the

others. "We have nothing else that the man could use, and for once I take the responsibility."

Smyrill was untied, leaping upon Olav and whining to show his joy, and the two groups parted, all heavily loaded with meat. The Skraelings now resumed their interrupted journey.

"Good day, friends," said Shakaka in her Greenland Norse, and Ohenaw repeated "friends." Then they were gone, and the others turned their faces toward the river again.

"We shall have a tale to tell," said Benedikt. "What a day's hunting! I never saw such herds or dreamed of them. What barns they would require, Ulf! What dairymaids to milk the cows! The farmer who bred such cattle would soon be rich."

"Or dead," said Ulf. "But it is a fine land, indeed. If we live to see Norway again, we shall have much to tell."

The four men walked with long shadows moving ahead of them, like four thin giants sliding over the prairie, and even tall Smyrill ran with his shadow to lead him. The Skraeling woman had made them packs which fastened across the forehead, and they walked with their heads bent down to carry the weight that rested below the shoulders.

"This is a good way to carry a heavy load, far better than a burden swinging from the hands or carried in a sack, first on one shoulder and then on another," said Ulf. "We must remember this when we get back to Norway."

"The word is *if*, my friend," said Benedikt. "Do you feel that you shall ever see Bergen again and the sea along the coast and the farms and the high fells? I do not. I try to imagine myself once more at Magnus Eirikson's court, and I cannot."

"It is the same with me," Ulf admitted, striding along with light step. "I think of my father's house and of the inns I knew and of the horse I rode and the girls I made love to, but I cannot imagine myself ever seeing any of them again."

"That is strange," said Olav. "I can see Hestnaes as though it were only last week that I was there, and I can feel Sokko's neck under my hand. When I close my eyes I see Ingrid at the door welcoming me as I ride up, and my mother smiling over her shoulder."

"And am I there?" Eirik asked. "No, I think I am not there when you imagine that scene."

Olav walked on without answering. Now that Eirik spoke of it, he realized that he had not imagined the Lapp at Sokka's head, holding the bridle rein, ready to lead the horse away to the barns. No, he had perhaps been too intent upon Ingrid, and thinking of her, the vision of Helga had naturally appeared with her. But whether anyone was at the horse's head or not, he had not thought. And now this seemed to him a disloyalty.

The sun was sinking all the time and the air had taken on a warm bright glow, almost red in color. The flowers that grew in the grass shone as though they were lighted candles, in particular a yellow daisy with a brown-black center, as dark as Olav's eyes.

They had walked some distance, and the loads on their backs seemed to grow heavier with every step.

"I should be glad to see the river," said Benedikt at last. "Where is it, anyway? We should be in sight of it by now."

"Yes," Eirik agreed. "I have been thinking for some time that we have been going in the wrong direction."

Ulf stopped and let his load slide to the ground, throwing back his head to ease his neck.

"We should have put Smyrill on our traces when we left the Skraelings," he said.

"It is late to think of that now," Benedikt retorted sharply. "You should have spoken of it at the time. But I suppose we were all excited by the meeting and the hunt and above all by the woman's cross. It seemed so easy then just to walk east to the camp. Eirik, you have a knowledge of hidden things, they say. Which direction should we take now? Where have we gone wrong?"

Eirik, who like the others, had taken off his pack, stood looking for a long time eastward. His small slanted eyes above their wide cheekbones were squinted into mere slits as he stared, swinging his head, now a little to the north, now a little to the south, murmuring under his breath. He was like the Knarr's weather vane, uncertain of the breeze. Everyone watched him in silence until he opened his eyes wider and nodded his head.

"Well?" asked Ulf.

Eirik pointed toward the northeast. "This country is strange to me," he said. "I cannot be sure as I am sure in Norway. But it feels best to me when I face in that direction."

"There is a rise of land with a sort of notch in it which we can use as a guide," Olav remarked, struggling back into his burden.

The light was growing very intense as the sun actually sank beyond the waves of grass. No one spoke of Paul, but everyone thought of him. He would be both angry and troubled. Never had any hunting party been delayed in its return beyond the sunsetting. Olav was growing tired, but he kept the pace set by Ulf's long

legs, walking with his forehead braced against the burden of meat, and his eyes for the most part fixed on
Eirik's heels moving ahead of him. They went on in this
way through the deepening fiery sunset light, in single
file, first Ulf, then Benedikt, then Eirik, and last Olav
with Smyrill sometimes following him, sometimes walking by his side.

The dog felt the men's uneasiness and shared it. He
no longer bounded through the long grasses, starting
up the great hares and dashing wildly off in beautiful
pursuit. He kept close to his master now, looking up
from time to time as though trying to read his face.
And now and then Olav gave him a word of encouragement.

They reached the top of one of the flower-capped
billows of grass, and Ulf stopped so suddenly that the
others, plodding on, walked into one another before
they realized that he had halted. Then they raised their
heads to look into the low wide hollow below them. In
the full glory of sunset a tree stood there, not such a
tree as the stunted willows by the spring, but a tall
solitary tree with wide branches and a great crest of
green leaves. Why it grew there, so far from other trees,
how it had grown so tall and vigorous, appeared a great
wonder. It was a greater wonder to see that all the
lower branches were hung with objects of different sorts
and that horned skulls, bleached white by the sun and
wind, surrounded its trunk in a circle. At any time the
tree would have been a rich and beautiful sight, but in
the intense light of sunset, it was like nothing which
the four men had ever seen before. If they had believed
in gods of the earth, this tree would have seemed like
such a god.

After the first surprised stare, they went on toward the tree, slowly and in silence, and as they approached it the sunset light moved upward, leaving the skulls and all the lower branches in shadow. As they came near, they saw that all sorts of offerings hung from the branches: thongs of deerskin, hung with bears' claws or teeth, clusters of clapperless bells made of soft copper, rattles of turtle shells, a white shed snakeskin torn a little now, antelope horns hanging together, and pouches of doeskin, painted in bold designs of red and white and yellow.

"This is a place very holy," said Eirik.

"I suppose the Skraelings come here," said Ulf. "I could use something like this," and before anyone could speak, the young man had reached in among the branches and brought out a particularly large and finely decorated pouch.

Olav felt his uneasiness increase, but it was Eirik who exclaimed, "Fool! Put the thing back! Quick! Do not hold it in your hand for an instant!"

And even Benedickt joined in, "Ulf, do as Eirik says!"

But Ulf was often headstrong and now he laughed loudly.

"Why should you all stand in awe of a tree and a lot of Skraeling gewgaws? I can find many uses for this," and laughing still, he opened the pouch and, tipping it upside down, emptied the contents into his left hand.

"Let us see what the wild men offer a tree," he went on, obstinately gay. "Dried leaves, well, they are fitting, and here are the beak and talons of an eagle, I take it, and more bears' claws and this is a little stone image of one of the creatures the Skraeling killed for us. Nothing I want. You may keep them, tree," and with another laugh, he threw the handful down with a thin clatter among the skulls.

The others stared at him, standing so insolently in the dark shadow of the evening branches, and as they stared, a sudden shivering shook the tree, and all the objects hanging from the boughs began to tinkle and jangle and rattle one against the other.

Even Ulf looked uneasy at last.

"Shall I hang up the pouch again, Eirik?" he asked in sudden meekness, like a child who admits a fault. But the Lapp turned away.

"It does not matter now," he answered indifferently, glancing neither at Ulf nor the tree, but with a hitch of his load, starting off again toward the northeast. The others followed in silence, Smyrill so close to Olav that at every step the dog nearly tripped him. And from behind them, low and insistent, sounded the wordless menacing voice of the tree.

Chapter 13
The Wolves Attack

FOR SOME TIME the party traveled in this manner, in silence. Soon they could no longer hear the tree, mourning perhaps, or was it invoking aid against them? They did not know. The sky had been green and rose; now it faded and darkened, and there was one great yellow star in the west when they looked over their shoulders and another great star like a drop of yellow fire overhead. They would be able to travel for another half-hour in the ashes of daylight. It was just possible that they might see Paul's campfire before night came on.

Olav felt a change in Smyrill. The dog had pricked

up his ears, and was looking over his shoulder, growling with menace and perhaps a little fear.

"Smyrill hears something," he said to Eirik.

The Lapp grunted. "Yes. It is a wolf howling."

Olav listened, but could hear nothing except the whisper of the tall grasses as he moved through them and the thumping of his own heart.

Ulf heard the wolf before Olav did.

"It is the hunting cry," he said.

"Yes," replied Eirik, walking steadily onward, "it has been answered, as well."

Olav felt a cold question, but said nothing. Now he could hear a far-off howl, a lonely sound. A little later he could hear it much more clearly, and a second voice, faint as the first had been. He knew that the animal was nearer, but as no one spoke, he too said nothing.

"There are seven or eight of them now, answering back and forth," Ulf said behind him. "What are they hunting, Eirik?" The Lapp walked steadily onward.

After a while he said, "They are hunting us, Ulf."

Benedikt spoke up for the first time.

"If we are the game, I say that it is time to prepare to meet these fellows. I am the last man and I do not relish the idea of having a wolf jump on my back."

"How do we prepare?" Eirik asked. "I still hoped we might come to Paul's fire, but there is no sign of it."

"There are four of us," said Ulf. "We can stand back to back for a while at least. But I grant you that it will not be an easy thing to fight by starlight."

"There is Smyrill," said Olav.

Ulf laughed. "The dog will be down and torn apart in the first onslaught. No, we with our axes are likely to last longer than Smyrill. I wish, friends, I had left that pouch in the tree."

Benedikt had taken off his load and turned now to smile at Ulf.

"Think no more of it, Ulf. Tree or no tree, the wolves were likely to come upon our tracks and the smell of good meat. What say you, Eirik, shall we leave the meat and go on without it? Do you think that they might delay over it while we got away?"

"A wolf's delay is of short duration," declared Eirik. "I cannot figure out how Olav is to escape this trap. How we three others might die is easy enough to see, but Gudrid in Greenland said that one should live."

Ulf groaned.

"The fault is mine, whatever you say, Benedikt. A good friend have you been, even now when you might have blamed me. If only the cursed tree were here, so that we might build a fire!"

"Yes," said Eirik, "a fire would save us."

They had put their burdens down all together in a heap of carrying skins and meat, and as Olav laid his with the others he felt the strong coarse grass under his hands. "Could we set the grass on fire?"

The howling was nearer now; it came from a dozen different points, but the wolves had slowed down. They were gathering their pack.

"We could try," said Eirik.

They all four brought out their fire steels and began to strike sparks. Every now and then one or another would succeed in starting a small tongue of flame among the dry grasses close to the ground, but each time the fire wavered, weakened and went out. Olav was angry with himself because he managed the steel so badly in the dark. His hands were clumsy. He kept listening for the wolves.

"God be praised, this burns!" Ulf exclaimed beyond him. Olav looked with the others. It was not a flame like a fire made of leaves or wood, but there was indeed a smoldering red rosette on the ground, growing brighter as they watched.

"Quick, it is the old dung of the humped cattle! Gather as much as we can before the wolves get here. The dung is everywhere."

Ulf's voice had regained its assurance. "Come on, you farm boys!" he shouted, beginning to pile up the dried cakes near his small fire. The others joined in, feeling about in the half darkness along the ground.

Eirik said, "We will build another fire to protect our other flank. Olav, tie up Smyrill now. If he runs out, they will rip him open in a second."

They lighted the second fire from the first. The dung was slow to catch. It was hard to have patience, hearing the howls so close. By now it was pitch black except for the starlight and the low smoky glow of the two fires. The men kept on feverishly gathering the fuel, stooping over, feeling for it, putting it into their cloaks. They dared not stop until Olav, raising his head, looked into two glowing eyes not ten feet away. He backed hastily between the fires and called the others in. By the time they had arranged themselves, Eirik and Olav side by side, with Benedikt and Ulf facing in the other direction, there was a ring of eyes all about them. The wolves were as silent as the stars overhead, which, often, like the wolves' eyes, seemed to shine in pairs. The pack was evidently surprised by the fires. They moved about in a wide circle, staring at the twin flames which also seemed like a pair of glowing and smoking eyes.

Olav leaned down to put more chips on the fire beside him, but Eirik spoke quickly.

"A night has many hours, Olav. Our fuel must last. See if you can make Smyrill be still. Each minute of delay is one minute nearer dawn."

The wolves slowly drew in as they became more accustomed to the fire, but when at last Eirik gave the order to put on more fuel they drew back a little again.

"This is cursed uneasy waiting," said Ulf. "I am going to sit down. There will be time enough to get to my feet if they spring."

"I am not so sure," Benedikt rejoined, "but sure or not, my legs grow weary of standing. What say you, Eirik? Shall we sit?"

Without any word said, the young men had turned to Eirik for leadership, and now the Lapp replied, "We will take turns. One will stand while the others sit. They seem in no hurry out there. Olav, sit with the others, but keep your ax in your right hand."

At the movement among the men the eyes stirred and then became fixed again. Once a pair moved forward, but when Eirik yelled and waved his arms, the eyes retreated again.

"Let us sing," said Eirik. "Whatever seems strange to them, makes them hesitate."

So for a long time the four men sang. Eirik's voice was no better than a crow's, but Benedikt had a beautiful clear voice and later he sang by himself the tale of the young hero, Fridthjof, of how he had loved his foster sister, a king's daughter, and of how, while he was away on his ship, she had been given in marriage to an old king.

Olav knew the tale. He had heard it sung at Hestnaes

and at the court when King Magnus and his queen sat at the high table and listened. But never had it sounded so beautiful as now when Benedikt sang it in the circle of wolves.

Fridthjof returned from three years' voyage and learned that his love was now married against her will. He dressed in rags and came as a beggar to the old king's court, but when one of the serving men made sport of him, he threw the man head over heels onto the floor, and his rags were torn open and Fridthjof appeared as a warrior, with gold bands upon his arms.

Then the old king called him to come to talk with him and gave him ale and pledged his health, but the young queen turned away her head and would not give him a glance. Ring, the old man, insisted that the young man should pass the winter at court and once, when a sleigh with the king and queen in it broke through the ice, it was Fridthjof who saved them. But still the queen would not give him a look or a word.

A wolf made a sudden leap inward between the fires, and Eirik stirred as quickly.

As the creature leaped into the light, a great gray-black shape, Eirik's ax landed squarely on the flat head and the wolf dropped down, twitching and jerking. Eirik caught it by the feet and threw it back among the others, who despatched it among snarlings and snappings.

"Go on, Benedikt," Eirik said as the sounds died away. "Now it is that you come to that part of Fridthjof's saga which most proved him a man."

And Benedikt sang on as though there had been no interruption, telling of how the old king, when the springtime came, went hunting and took Fridthjof with him. In the midst of the woods Ring said that he was tired and would sleep a little. So he lay down and fell asleep with his head on Fridthjof's knee.

Then a bird sang, "Now is your chance, now is your chance, no one is near."

And another bird sang, "You cannot betray him."

And Fridthjof, deeply torn in spirit, rose and took off his sword and hung it on a tree in the thicket, out of his own reach.

But soon the old king opened his eyes and told him that he had seen everything.

"I knew from the first minute that I saw you who you were and for what you had come. But you and Ingeborg have held yourselves nobly in all things. What you did not know is that I am dying, and to you I leave my kingdom and my queen."

"Ah," said Ulf when the last note died away, "that was a fine gift finely won and finely given. I wonder now what our friends the wolves make of the saga?"

It seemed almost as if the circle of eyes had enjoyed the singing for, as Benedikt fell silent, they became restless and began to pad about again in their circle.

"They go widdershins," said Eirik, "from east to north to west to south as is the custom with witches and warlocks. But the stars that were just over the tops of the grass when the night began are a man's height up in the heavens now. We are that much nearer the dawn. Sing again, Benedikt."

Benedikt laughed.

"You would think, Eirik, to hear you, that I was a water mill to keep clacking on hour after hour. But my throat rebels. Someone else will have to sing to our friends out there."

"Tell us a story, Eirik," said Olav. "Talk seems to

be as much to their taste as singing. I will stand now
and you sit and tell us about the wizards of Lapland."

"As you wish," said Eirik, and his voice sounded
pleased. "But first put another chip on the fire, and
wait until the edges begin to catch before you put it
down, or it may go out. And then we should have little
more chance for story-telling."

Eirik's voice was harsh, but it had a curious stirring
quality to it and as he settled himself and began to
speak, it almost seemed to Olav as though the wolves
were thinking, "We will listen to this tale first and then
we will make our kill. Dead men tell no stories."

"Long ago in my country," Eirik began, as he had
begun so many stories at Hestnaes when Olav was a
little boy, "long ago when the world was new, there
were two wizards and one was old and one was young.

"And the old wizard took some new-fallen snow and
from it he made a woman and he built her a house and
she lived in it.

"Both the old wizard and the young wizard wished
to marry the woman who was very beautiful. So they
competed before her to show their power.

"The old wizard said, 'Fire is the most powerful of
the elements,' and he seized a brand from the fire and
hurled it into the skies, which in those days were black
without any light. And for many hours the brand
circled across the heavens, lighting them, and at last it
fell into the sea, throwing up many beautiful sparks.
And then there was darkness again.

"The young wizard looked about for what he could
find to light up the skies and he found a piece of ice
that covered the top of the well which he had dug
beside the house. It was round and smooth and not
very thick and when he had thrown it into the air it

gave forth a pale white light, and it too crossed the heavens and disappeared. Then in the east the firebrand reappeared, and after it was gone, the disk of ice. This went on for a long time, but the ice grew thin and melted slowly away. As it melted, more and more frost flowers appeared in the sky.

"But the woman could not choose between them.

"Then the old wizard made the earth, and he called the four winds and gave them seeds. They scattered the seeds of the grass and the grains and from them the cattle were born and the old wizard said, 'This is good.'

"And he called the woman and gave her meat and cheese and bread and ale.

"But the young wizard summoned the winds and gave them the seeds of flowers, which were all that were left, and they planted them over the world, and from them there were born the butterflies and bees. The young wizard took a honeycomb and gave it to the woman, and she ate and again she could not choose between them.

"Then the old wizard was angry with her and he said in a loud voice. 'Choose me, for I gave you life.'

"And the young wizard said, 'I have given you nothing but a kiss.'

"And at that the woman said that she chose the young wizard, and they were the first man and woman."

"Sira Andres tells the story rather differently," Ulf said with a laugh. "But your tale is a good tale, Eirik, and no one will deny that women today are still much like the first woman, and will choose the young man with a bold swing to his cloak over the old merchant with a heavy moneybag."

"The frost flowers have swung up in the heavens a little farther," said Benedikt. "Would, Eirik, that the

ice disk were with them tonight so that we might see
more of our guests. They are growing restless again."

Eirik was in high good humor, pleased by the old
tale he had told.

"Let us all get to our feet and sally suddenly among
them. But mind you, only ten steps. Strike if you can,
but then return immediately. Let nothing delay you,
but it would be as well for these dogs to be less certain
of our gentleness."

Olav held Smyrill close beside him on a thong and,
at a shout from Eirik, ran out, yelling, his ax held over
his head to strike. But the wolves melted before him
and he remembered Eirik's warning and dragged
Smyrill back again to the fire, laughing with the excitement and the relief of action.

"I hit only air," said Eirik.

"And I too," said Benedikt.

But Ulf declared that he had felt something under
his ax and that the creature had howled. Still, it could
not have been badly wounded, for the others did not
fall upon it and kill it as they had Eirik's wolf.

"It is enough to make them doubt," Eirik declared.
"Oh, if we but had a lighted branch now, we should set
them running as we did the musk oxen in Greenland!
But we cannot even throw some of this lighted dung
among them; we cannot afford to waste it before dawn."

"We haven't so much as a spear with us," said Ulf,
and that gave him an idea. He fastened a long thong
to his dagger and amused himself by throwing it out
toward the wolves and drawing it back again by the
thong. The eyes retreated, not caring for this game,
but after a while the thong broke, and he was forced
to give over his play. But it had amused them all
and kept them awake, and one constellation, like a

twice-broken stick, which had been low in the east, was now in the very zenith.

"We are more than halfway to the dawn," said Eirik, "and they are not finding us such tender meat as they drooled for at sundown."

"Do you notice," asked Olav, "that one of them has only one eye? I have been watching them. That one eye hangs higher in the air than any of the others. It must belong to a very large wolf."

"I too have been watching that eye," said Ulf. "Unless I am mistaken, it belongs to the leader of the pack. When it begins its warlock pacings about the fire, all the other eyes begin to move, and when it is still, they are still."

"Odin." Benedikt's voice sounded sleepy, and now he yawned. "An Odin of the wolves. And like the god, he doubtless sacrificed that eye in return for wisdom."

"It is time you took your turn to stand guard, Benedikt," said Eirik. "If you do not look out, you will think yourself back at Bergen, sleeping among the feathers. And you will wake to find your Odin at your throat. He is the one to watch. The stars do not seem to me as bright as they were, and it is growing colder. The dawn must be almost here, and I think before it comes, they will try to root us out of shelter."

"Eirik, you are overfearful. The brutes haven't budged for an hour."

"All the more reason for them soon to take the kinks out of their legs. I was afraid you were too courtly for this kind of business."

Benedikt laughed. "If Magnus could see us now!"

Stretching, he rose to his feet, and his twin shadows moved out among the wolves, which drew back a little, and then returned.

Ulf remarked, "But you are not sitting down, Eirik."

"I am not tired."

"Still, it is your turn."

"I shall not insist upon it. What I wish to bring through this night more than anything else is a whole skin."

"Let him be, Ulf," Benedikt broke in. "Who ever could convince a Lapp?"

"One-Eye is beginning to walk again." The voice was Olav's.

"But he has come no nearer," said Ulf.

Suddenly there was a din of steel upon steel. The eyes leaped backward into the darkness. Their stare shone phosphorescent with surprise.

"Enough," shouted Eirik above the noise. "Never give them a chance to grow accustomed to anything. That was well thought of, Olav."

Olav, feeling his way, sheathed his dagger and sword and picked up the ax again.

"They are easily beguiled," he said. "Did you see One-Eye? He must have jumped three feet backward in his track."

Benedikt's voice came from above. He seemed to tower into the darkness like a giant, his feet and ankles and the bottom of his cloak dimly lighted by the fires, his head a shadow against the stars.

"If I am to keep awake," the voice said, "someone must tell a tale. Ulf, it is your turn."

"I do not know any sagas, not having been at court."

"As though sagas were told only at court! Nonsense, man, do not pretend shyness at this late hour. If you have no sagas at the tip of your tongue, tell us something of your own adventures. Or have you had none, never having been at court?"

Ulf laughed and the eyes wavered and were still.

"Yes, I have had adventures, never having been at
court. And the strangest happened to me on the night
that I killed a man. He was not one whom I had ever
liked. I felt no regret as I wiped my sword on the grass
and started up the steep path which led over the hills
to my own place, yet neither was I happy about what
had happened. It was I who had in some sort brought
on the quarrel, and now that the ale flowed less warmly
through my veins, I wished that it had been he who
had said the first jeering word. And then I thought, ten
minutes ago that big fellow was drinking from the horn
and stretching his feet to the fire and what and where
is he now? You do not think such thoughts after a
battle, but here we had been together at one fire with
the same wench serving us ale from the same brown
jug. It was a different thing altogether from battle.

"And I knew, besides, that he had many friends and
that things would go hard with me at the gathering of
the people.

"So as I climbed the steep path out of the valley, I
was in no happy frame of mind. There was a moon in
the sky, a waning moon with a hangdog air, and I
thought its light worse than none. Yet when the clouds
threw their rags across it, I did not like that either, and
was glad when the poor thing struggled free.

"You know the paths under the fells, how lonely they
are. The huts of those who tended the cattle were still
far above me. There was not a Christian soul within
five miles. That night the fells seemed to crouch against
the sky, and the trees, when I had to walk through
stretches of them, seemed to be saying, 'There he goes,
the killer, there he goes,' and although I know it is
impossible, yet it seemed to me as though the trees

followed me along the path and crowded nearer to have a good look at me.

"I was anxious to be rid of them, I can tell you, yet when I came out into the open land it was worse still. For one thing, I could see the moon more clearly, and somehow I got it into my head that the clouds meant to do it harm, and it seemed to be running from them. When the darkness brought it down, I felt that it was I who had been overtaken, and when it struggled free, I sweated with relief. Why should I have imagined such things, Benedikt, think you?"

"Sick fancies come to a man in sorrow," came Benedikt's voice from above, but Eirik said, "In our country, the spirits of the just-killed may ride the killer, and often enough drive him over a cliff or into deep water."

"It may be indeed that I was corpse-ridden that night. I longed to return to the valley, but it was filled with his friends, so I knew that I must keep on. In one place the path lay between two tall rocks and the spot is called The Door. As I came nearer to these rocks I grew more and more afraid—why I do not know. I had often passed between them, with no thought. But the people going to the upper pastures leave presents on them both, a small cheese, or a basket of berries. And I had heard stories of their behavior on Midsummer's Eve and had laughed at them.

"But this night I did not laugh."

"One-Eye is moving again," interrupted Olav.

"Yes," came Eirik's voice, "put a little more fuel on the fire, Olav, and I will do the same for this one."

"There is very little left."

"But we cannot let the fires go out. Have you enough there to last until dawn?"

"How soon will dawn come? There is very little."

"Put on one piece. We must act from minute to minute. When we can no longer feed the fires perhaps we will find something else to do. At least we will hear the end of Ulf's story first. Rattle your sword and dagger again, Olav. That keeps the brutes still for a little. Let's have no more interruptions. There, well done, Black-Brow. They have drawn back again."

"But not so far this time."

"No, a charm soon wears thin," said Eirik. "As we listen we must be thinking of new tricks. I can feel the dawn wind now along the grass."

"Hush there, and let Ulf tell his tale. You said, Ulf, that you were in no laughing mood as you drew near the rocks."

"No. I who laugh at most things, did not laugh that night. The moon was sometimes shining and sometimes, as I have told you, it was strangled under clouds. Sometimes I could see the rocks far off above me on the hillside and sometimes I could not see them at all. I do not know which way was worse. They had a waiting look, as though they knew very well who was approaching them and what he had done. If there had been any way around the rocks, be sure I should have taken it, but the slope at that spot is very steep and broken, and the only path is between.

"As I drew near, the moon came out suddenly and it was as though the rocks stopped some movement that they had begun. I was so frightened that I became brave again. It is like a second wind when one is running. I threw back my cloak on my shoulders and I eyed the two big masses of stone and they eyed me back again, although they had no eyes.

"I think I was smiling then. 'I'll run for it,' I said to myself or to them, it was all the same, and I dug my toes into the ground and I ran straight for The Door, without giving them any more time to consider. The moon burned clear as a well-lighted torch, and by its light I saw the rocks closing in. But they had waited a moment too long. I felt their weight against my shoulders, but I slipped through. It was only my cloak that they closed in upon, nipping it so hard that the clasp at my throat was torn open, and I ran on, leaving it to them. A friend of mine found it on the path next day, as though I had dropped it. But the pin which had held it was bent almost double."

Ulf stopped speaking, and his silence might have been an agreed-upon signal, for at the moment his voice died away, the one-eyed wolf, which was on the side guarded by Olav and Eirik, sprang forward, followed by six or seven others, charging between the two low fires. Olav saw them coming and got to his feet, but he would have been too late if Smyrill had not been there, snarling and snapping like a devil, giving Olav the necessary extra seconds that he needed. The wolves on Ulf's and Benedikt's side came closer but did not close in. Ulf had time to reach his feet and join in the battle. The wolves fought, leaping for the men's throats, or slashing sideways with their great jaws, trying to cut the tendons under their quarry's knees. The men struck with their battle-axes. Only Eirik had a chance to use the sword in his left hand. Before the battle had really begun, it was over, and the wolves had burst through and joined the rest of the pack on the other side, leaving their dead and wounded behind. It was light enough so that Olav could just make out their shapes, one lying still, and one trying to crawl away, which Eirik finished with a

blow on the head. Another wolf Smyrill had by the
throat. It was still growling and twisting its long jaws
for a hold, and Olav took careful aim and finished
Smyrill's kill.

Eirik threw them, all three, out to the pack which
breakfasted at leisure and then trotted off without more
than a casual glance at the men, the big one-eyed wolf
in the lead.

"Ah, ha!" Eirik taunted them. "You found us a
harder nut to crack than you counted on this night.
Remember it, next time you come on the tracks of
men."

"They look like big dogs," said Benedikt. "Handsome, too. And what a bite the creatures have! One
went for my knee and bruised me well through cloak
and robe and stocking. How has Smyrill fared, Olav?"

"Not too badly," said Olav. "He is cut about the
neck, but not deeply. God be praised they did not break
his legs. Look how pleased with himself he is! He has
wanted to fight with a wolf ever since we reached this
land, and now at last he has done it."

"Even the morning star has faded away now," said
Eirik. "In half an hour our shadows will join us. We
had better sit down and eat our own breakfast."

"Not so close to the wolves' breakfast," Benedikt
protested. "You may say that being at court has made
me squeamish, but I should prefer to eat on the far side
of the rise. I shall have a better appetite."

Olav felt the same way, and although Ulf and Eirik
laughed at them, they were not unwilling to move on.
All, including Smyrill, felt proud to have lived through
that night and they sat at ease in the soft long grass and
ate with good appetite, living over again the adventures
of the evening.

"I shall never see stars again without remembering their eyes," said Olav.

"There were times when I should not have wagered much on our chances of seeing stars again," Ulf declared between bites. "What a land this is! Here one feels oneself a man."

Benedikt leaned back on his elbows, smiling at Ulf.

"Telling stories all night in a circle of wolves may make you feel like a man, friend. Me it makes sleepy."

"We had better get back to camp as soon as we can," said Eirik. "Paul will be sending out men to look for us. The more we are delayed, the angrier he will be. I doubt if he slept last night more than did we."

"Yes," said Benedikt, "even I say Paul is a good leader and has the lives of his people on his heart. And for a Swede to say that of a Norwegian, is praise indeed."

Ulf laughed. "Why so it is! I had forgotten that you were a Swede."

"And I suppose you mean that for praise indeed."

But Eirik would give the young men little time for their jests and raillery. Frowning, he looked eastward again.

"Where is that notched slope?"

Olav joined him. "It was over there last evening."

"I do not see it now."

"Can it be that we have passed it?"

"I should not say so."

But they looked northward and then behind them. They did not see the notch, but they did see something else.

A white thin column of smoke was rising against the blue sky to the west.

"Skraelings," said Eirik under his breath. "Do they

see our smoke? You two by the fire, beat it out quickly. There are others behind us."

"Perhaps Shakaka and Ohenaw," Benedikt suggested comfortably, but he helped Ulf stamp out the small fire of dung over which they had cooked their meat.

"No, there is a second smoke," said Eirik.

"It is like an answer," Olav murmured, "as when last night the second wolf answered the first."

A third pillar of smoke rose, miles away from the other two.

"I do not like these signals," said Ulf uneasily. "Who are these people and what have they to say to one another? Has it anything to do with us?"

"How can I know everything!" snapped Eirik. "But I do not like it either. Now, what in the name of St. Olav are they doing?"

The first column of smoke had suddenly been quenched, then it rose again briefly, was quenched, rose for about the same time, was quenched and then rose steadily once more like the trunk of a tree, dissolving into branches and hazy filaments in the breeze of the upper air.

"Look at the second one," said Benedikt. "It is behaving in the same way."

"I think they are covering and uncovering the fire with a wet hide," Ulf mused. "But why?"

"They are speaking to one another. Of so much I am certain. There goes the third fire and already the first is answering."

"I would give a year of my life to know what they are saying," grumbled Ulf.

"Have any of us a year of life to give?" Eirik demanded. "This is worse than the wolves by far." He had become melancholy again: all his recent energy was drawn in upon himself in gloomy meditation. Olav knew Eirik's black moods. While he was in one, he cared nothing for the world outside his thoughts. So far as he was concerned, they might all stand there waiting for their fate to come upon them.

But Olav was not for nothing Sigurd's son. Somewhere deep in him, deep as his bones and sinews, were the leader's steadiness, the leader's sense of responsibility.

"The fires are a long way off," he said cheerfully, "and for all we know we may be very near the river by now. We bring good meat with us and better news of the Skraeling woman who wears a cross. Let us put our foreheads under the leather straps again, and be on our way, foster father."

It was a name he rarely used. Eirik was not his foster father, yet the affection between them was of that order, and at the word, the Lapp roused from his gloom to give Olav a deep brooding look.

"Let us go, as you say, Olav," he replied with a kind of humbleness, and the four men helped one another into their burdens, and without another glance at the three smoke pillars, still in silent consultation behind them, started off toward the east, this time led by Olav.

Chapter 14

Pursuit

ALL MORNING they walked and still they did not find the river. Still the plain stretched about them, with its waving grass and surf of flowers. Somewhere they had gone wrong, but they did not know how to correct their mistake. Once a herd of animals, swift and brightly colored, with small horns, somewhat like deer and somewhat like goats, sprang past them. When they seemed to be gone, they circled back, bounding lightly through the tall grasses, to stand at some distance and stare at the men, then circled farther, and stared once more.

"They are like porpoises playing about the Knarr," said Olav. "This land is as much like the sea as land."

They had stopped to rest for a few minutes as they watched the leaping goat-deer, and for once Smyrill was so stiff and weary that he was easily called back from the chase. Ulf, standing at ease, became aware of the painted pouch still swinging from his belt and made as though to untie it.

"Let it be," said Benedikt. "It is the spoil that we carry back. We do not admit defeat."

"What say you, Eirik?" asked Ulf, with that docility which alternated with his fits of headstrong exuberance when he would listen to no one's advice.

The little Lapp looked at the pouch darkly and shook his head.

"It is as Benedikt says. The harm has been done, I think. We have not come to the end of it. But throwing away the pouch would make no difference. Keep it, and pray that you may live to wear it into camp."

"Oh, as for that," said Benedikt lightly, "a man must die sometime!" And he began to sing the eleventh Rune of Odin, in his fine voice.

"If I shall to battle
Lead my old friends,
I sing under the shields,
And they go with might
Safe to the fray,
Safe out of the fray,
Safe wherever they come from."

The goat-deer had at last bounded off, and Eirik began to get into his pack.

"Stay," said Ulf. "While we are here, why don't we eat? It will lighten our packs."

"A good thought," Benedikt chimed in. "It is a marvel how much meat we eat at a sitting, now that we have no bread or curds to eat with it. I, too, Ulf, would gladly carry some of this load in my belly," and he reached for his fire steel.

But Olav remembered the three talking fires behind them, which had made the same shivers go down his back as had the wolves' calls answering one another through the dusk the evening before.

"No, no fire, Benedikt. We don't want to beckon any of the wild men to us like that."

"No doubt they could track us, if they wished."

"But at least that takes time and they would have to come upon our trail somewhere. It is a narrow thing in this great place. But our smoke—isn't that true, Eirik?"

"To light a fire is to court death," said Eirik with finality. "Are you so nice, Benedikt, that you cannot touch raw meat? Until we get back to the others, it is raw meat or a tightened belt, friend."

Benedikt glanced at Ulf.

"I can take as much raw meat as a Norwegian," he wagered. "But you are not in on this, Eirik. A Lapp is a different matter. For all I know, you were bred on raw meat."

The four undid their packs and drew their daggers, but only Eirik and Smyrill enjoyed the meal. Little enough the others took. Benedikt needed to eat only a small piece to have taken as much as the Norwegians, and more he could not.

They were tying up the skin again when suddenly Ulf said, shading his keen eyes with his hand, "What in the name of God is that over yonder?"

All straightened up, still on their knees, and looked

back in the direction from which they had come. The clear morning had turned to a cloudy noon, as often happened in this country. Not that the clouds obscured the sun. It still shone brightly on everything so that the tops of the clouds were white as foam on blue-purple bases against a blazing blue sky, and their shadows lay like slowly moving herds across the waving grass and flowers, so that the darkness made the brightness brighter still.

In the midst of these great flat expanses of limitless plains and limitless skies, one upright figure appeared, something thin and very tall, stretching up from the earth toward the clouds.

"What is it?" Ulf asked. "I have never seen its like."

"It is coming toward us," Benedikt added quietly.

"See," said Ulf, "it dances as it comes. It spins round and round upon itself."

"But still it is coming toward us," Olav muttered. "Eirik, what is it?"

"Some wizard of the country has taken this form," Eirik answered in an unshaken voice, although Olav, looking toward him, saw that he was shivering. "He has made himself tall so that he may see us at a great distance. I think he has taken the form of the wind."

Benedikt said suddenly, "I think it is nothing but a kind of whirlpool of air, such as the whirlpools we have seen in water, but much greater, perhaps born of the heat on these meadows at noon, and it moves with the current of the wind."

"Yet we feel no wind," said Eirik, "and in all the great swing of the horizon, it has chosen to come toward us."

Olav got to his feet, his load of meat dangling from one hand.

"We must do something. Let us move quickly toward the south, so that it may pass us by."

"Do you suppose that the thing will not follow?" Eirik demanded. "If it has traced us for miles, will it be put off because we run a few yards?"

Benedikt sided with Olav.

"It can do no harm to move, Eirik. Two of us can go north and two south."

"And be hunted down separately!" scoffed Eirik. "No, if we are to be slain by a wizard of air, let us all die together at least. But if you wish, we will walk toward the south," and, picking up his burden, he joined the others, all on their feet by now.

Trying not to run, their heads turned toward the approaching marvel, they hurried through the long grasses. The shadow of one of the clouds now lay over them, but the revolving figure was bright in a shaft of sunlight. It seemed the color of dust, with perhaps a faintly greenish tinge, thicker than air, and yet like spinning air. It moved very deliberately, and yet it moved, and always toward them.

Eirik threw down his pack.

"It does no good to run away," he cried to the others. "Let us die facing it. The wizard shall not be able to tell that we Norsemen ran like rabbits."

"You speak for us all," said Ulf. "Let us draw our swords, friends, and go forward to meet it."

"As you will," said Benedikt. "I still believe it is but some strange eddy."

"Will it kill us the less?" Ulf demanded. "Wizard or eddy, it means to overtake us, and we must meet it as best we may."

"Wait—" said Eirik. "After all, I too know something of wizardry. If you have prayers to say, now is the time to say them, but I shall call upon the old gods."

The Lapp's face looked like stone, except where his small hooded eyes glistened between their lids. He bent forward, muttering to himself; tearing away the grass, he took some of the earth into his hand, and with it the head of a yellow flower, and two perfect blades of grass, and a crumble of the dried dung, intoning all the time. When he had taken a small part of everything about him, he made a motion to the others to stay back. Olav put his hand on Smyrill's collar to restrain him, but the dog had no desire to leave his master.

All alone, Eirik advanced, a small bandy-legged figure, his wide-cheeked, scraggly-bearded head held high, facing the tall whirling apparition which advanced with a roaring sound. When no more than twenty feet separated them, he shouted something in a language, not Norse, and holding the palm of his hand to his mouth, blew the dust, flower head, dried dung and grasses toward the swaying giant of air.

The thing whirled round and round three or four times, more and more slowly. Suddenly there was a shower of dust and broken grass blades from the air and the monster was gone, vanished as though it had never been.

The three watchers were left agape with surprise. The apparition had been so inhumanly terrifying, and now it was no more than a pricked bladder.

"I told you that it was a tall eddy of air," Benedikt repeated, rather loudly.

"If it was, man, it would have killed us none the less. How do you explain its yielding to Eirik's magic?" Ulf demanded.

"Even before Eirik went to meet the thing, it seemed to me that it was beginning to run down like a boy's top."

"Nonsense. In another minute we should have been spinning with it—men, boy, dog, meat and all. Eirik, Benedikt has learned so much at court that he has not even sense enough to know when to be grateful. But I am only a houseless outlaw, so I thank you for saving our lives."

"And I too, my Eirik," Olav said. "If I must die in this place, I would rather die under the teeth of wolves than be carried off by a wizard of air."

Eirik looked at them benignly. "I saved my own skin as well as yours," he said. "You owe me no thanks. But, Ulf, yours are the keenest eyes. Am I right in thinking that the thing has a mate and that it is following to see what has happened to the first one?"

Ulf turned unwillingly westward again. Small and finer than a raised finger, a second something far, far off was astir where they had first seen the other.

"Do you know what I think?" Benedikt asked excitedly. "I think that there is a river over there along which, for some reason, the eddies are born, and then they pick up the earth for their bodies from the river banks."

"And for some reason follow us wherever we go," Ulf joined in. "Oh, Benedikt, you talk nonsense."

"This time I am only a little afraid," Olav interrupted. "If Eirik could dispel one wizard, he can dispel another."

Eirik said nothing. He was muttering to himself, his eyes fixed upon the approaching figure, and took no part in the talk, which came disjointedly, after long silences from the others as they stood watching.

"This one moves more to and fro," Benedikt remarked.

"As though it were hunting for its mate," Ulf added.

There was again a long silence while the thing drew nearer and larger, sometimes in sunshine, sometimes dark with shadow, spinning always, but now standing almost in one place and now moving rapidly, but in a more aimless fashion than the other had shown. Still in a general way, it was coming in their direction.

"But it seems blind," Olav said. "Not like the other."

Ulf put his finger to his lip and shook his head, and after that they stood in silence, though several times Benedikt clearly wished to speak. By now the apparition was quite near them, but it seemed smaller than the first, and perhaps of divided purpose. Olav thought that it might be more anxious to find its companion than to find them. It wavered and swayed, its upper part bending like a dancer's. It had a peculiar grace, and seemed to him dangerous but a little pathetic, as though this were a witch in search of her lost warlock. Whatever it may have been, whether a natural thing as Benedikt clearly still believed, or a magical shape as the others thought, it passed them by, a hundred yards away, and wavered eastward until it too disappeared.

They saw no more of these wanderers anywhere. The plains which had spawned the two presences lay, to all appearances, peacefully empty.

"In heaven's name, let us get back to Paul," Ulf exclaimed. "When it comes to terror, there is nothing to choose between rock and air, but at least I was soon through The Door. What I want now is to feel twenty-nine men around me and to be square in the middle of them for a while, with the others on the outside."

Even Eirik laughed. He had laid down the things he had again gathered in his hand, and his soul had come back into his body. His eyes had their old sardonic smiling look.

"And where do we find Paul, friend?" he asked good-humoredly. "One thing I do see, there are low hills beginning to appear over there."

"Yes, and they are wooded hills, too, God be praised," Ulf said. "I shall be thankful not to see so far."

"But we did not leave Paul and the others in the woods," Benedikt argued reasonably. "They are somewhere this side of the hills."

"I have found the slope with the notch in it again," Olav exclaimed pointing. "That was our landmark. Shall we go in that direction, Eirik?"

Eirik faced where Olav pointed, and again he seemed to withdraw the human and thinking elements from his body. Only some strange impersonal force remained, swinging him slowly in a quarter arc and at last bringing him back where he had begun.

He said nothing, but nodded, and this time he knelt down and began to arrange the carrying pack on his forehead once more. Olav hurried to help him. He felt warmly grateful to Eirik for his many wisdoms. No wonder Sigurd had kept him always by his side and trusted his advice more than that of any other man. With Eirik, one was safe.

Yet Sigurd's grave was in the tides. When death comes at an appointed time, no skill, no wisdom, can turn him from the path.

But this was not the appointed time! Olav felt it to the marrow of his bones and a joy ran through all his body. The plains were so beautiful. Nothing could harm him on this bright-coated day. He and the others had

outfaced the wolves and the wizards. Whatever else
might happen, somehow they would find Paul and the
rest. As Ulf fitted the strap to Olav's forehead, the boy
was singing,

"It is better to be merry
Than to be downhearted
Whatever may come to hand."

As usual in this land, it was hard to judge distances.
They came to the rise with the notch in it sooner than
they had expected, nor did they find what they had
expected, for that had only been a falling away of the
land.

Ulf spoke for them all.

"I want no more marvels!" he exclaimed. "Tree,
wolves and wizards and now this! We are bewitched.
I will not look at it."

Benedikt laughed.

"A marvel it is, but it does not look to be one that
can hurt us. There is nothing living to be seen except
butterflies, and those surely an outlaw need not fear.
Come, summon up your courage, man! Let's see what
new wonder is here."

"How can this be Skraeling work?" Olav asked.

"It might be something that their gods have made,"
Eirik said darkly.

"Let us leave without looking further," Ulf urged
again.

But Benedikt held his cloak.

"You know as well as I do that you could not be
pulled away until we have made out this shape."

Still Ulf protested, "A storm is coming up. It is growing very dark."

Olav had already climbed the low grass-grown earth-
works, first slipping off his load.

"Could it be an old fort, Eirik?" he called down.

But Eirik shook his head.

"It is too low and too sloping and too large," he
replied. "Wait, I'll come up. What is that bulge to the
west?"

By now all four and Smyrill were on the earthworks.
It was Ulf who said: "Isn't that a snake's head with
the tail in its mouth? I have a silver brooch of much the
same design."

"It *is* a snake's head, as I live!" Benedikt exclaimed.
"All this that we are standing on is one great serpent,
swallowing its own tail. What would that mean, Eirik?"

"Did they not teach you at court?" Eirik asked.
"Where I was born, the snake with its tail in its mouth
stands for eternity. It is without beginning and without
end."

"But why should the wild men make such great
monuments?"

Eirik shrugged. "How should I know?"

Olav and Smyrill had already left the serpent body
and were climbing onto a strangely shaped mound
which the other mound encircled. A last gleam of sunlight struck across the boy as he stood shouting back
to the others.

"It's a turtle, four legs, tail and head! And the head
is facing east."

Eirik and the two young men joined him on the curve
of the turtle's back.

"These are mysteries," Eirik said. "I have heard men
declare that the world is held on a turtle's back. Yet how
should the Skraelings know that? If a wise man had
made this thing, I would say that it was a symbol of

earth, surrounded by space, but these people are savages. Could it be, as I first said, that their gods made it?"

"If it was made by gods, it is men who have kept the grass cropped on it. See those piles of dried grass over there," Benedikt pointed out. "This has the look of a sacred place."

"And all the time we linger here, Paul is growing angrier and angrier." Ulf clearly held to his first opinion of wishing no more to do with wonders than he could help. "There, I hear the chariot wheels of thunder again. Wasn't that a drop of rain? This is no spot where I wish to be caught by one of the storms of this land."

But willy-nilly, they *were* caught. They had half a dozen times experienced the country's great thunderstorms, but never one which came so quickly in such rivers of rain, blinding their eyes and beating down upon their heads. Lightning flared, crackling down all the sky and almost simultaneously the thunder drummed upon their ears.

They had no time to leave the back of the earthen turtle. Crouching together, with only the shelter of one another's bodies, they waited, while the lightning flickered about like a whip of fire searching them out. To right and left of them the lash blazed and crackled and the sound of the thunder was almost continuous. Olav crouched over the terrified Smyrill, shielding the dog as best he could under his cloak. He tried to close his eyes to the lightning, but the blinding flares struck through his eyelids and in terror he opened them again and crouched there, wincing and staring.

Twice he saw a fireball strike from the sky and run along the earth near them. The tall grasses were beaten down by the downpour, and the men were exhausted under the blows of the rain. But gradually the intervals between the thunder and lightning grew greater and the force of the rain lessened. The lightning was something which ran like a serpent down the sky, not a whip lashed over their shoulders. Little by little the men raised their heads, and wringing out their wet cloaks, wiped their wet faces and pushed back the hair plastered along their cheeks. Smyrill came out from their center and shook himself vigorously. It was still raining, but mildly now.

To the astonishment of the other men, Eirik laughed in a rusty crow. Olav could not remember ever before hearing him laugh aloud.

"We have survived the three ordeals," he boasted. "There is nothing more for us to fear. Now you shall see. In a little while we will find the camp."

Benedikt stood wringing out his clothes as best he could and grinning.

"What a lot of scarecrows! No sleep, no food, no rest! We look only fit to be stuck out in a field to frighten the birds."

Ulf shook himself much as Smyrill had done, and stretched his long arms.

"The sun is trying to shine," he yawned. "We will do well enough tomorrow. What a country, though! What a country!"

The air was cooler and smelled of the earth and the downtrodden grass. The raindrops hung everywhere and in the faint sunlight they trembled and glistened. When the men took up their loads again they seemed to be wading through seaweed, so wet was all that verdure. A bird flew out of some dripping grass cavern and mounted up, singing, into the sky.

Eirik again led the way. He had set his course by the direction of the turtle's head.

"We shall have no further trouble," he promised the others. "For a long time we must have been walking parallel to our river but now we shall come to it."

"If we are away for another night, we might better stay away for good than have to listen to what Paul will say," Ulf remarked cheerfully. "Have you noticed that he is limping these days?"

Eirik nodded. "An old wound, which he got at the Narrow Straits."

Then suddenly against the clearing sky they saw two or three white birds apparently flying over the plains.

"Gulls!" exclaimed Olav and at the sudden sound of his voice, Smyrill began to bark as though he gave a cheer.

Eirik quickened his swift pace and in five minutes they stood above the stream lined with sparse trees.

"We are so close to the hills now that the others must be down river from here," Eirik declared. "Come, friends, a little more and we can rest."

Paul heard their voices and came to meet them, his face at first alight, but then it clouded over and he drew his brows together and berated them. It was Olav who answered for the rest, saying little of the wolves and less of the other marvels, but telling in great detail of their meeting with the two savages. The other men crowded about listening, and greeted their story with great excitement. Nicolas burst into prayers of thanksgiving at hearing that a Skraeling had actually been seen wearing a cross, and Sira Andres joined him with more moderation. Paul acknowledged that this and the

Norse speech were wonderful matters, but he was not
pleased that the two had not been brought back for him
to question.

"I could have found out something," he insisted,
half-angrily.

"Did you wish us to tie them up with the meat on
our backs, or to bring them to you at sword's point,
Paul?" Ulf rallied him. "You may be sure that we tried
everything that could be tried. And you know that
Eirik is better at sign language and at making himself
understood than any of us. He got nowhere with them
and neither would you."

Paul shrugged impatiently. "Then I should have gone
with them, if I had had to travel by foot for days. For
all you know, they are going straight back to the Greenlanders. They were hunting. They could not have been
more than a few days' journey from their base. And
you! You let the opportunity slip through your fingers."

Eirik alone did not look at all crestfallen.

"What will be, will be, Paul Knutson. If we had not
come back, you would have been in a rare taking. This
Shakaka seemed to understand about the bracelet."

"Enough to put it on, no doubt, like any other
woman," said Johan, but not ill-humoredly.

They started upstream at first dawn the next morning
in a curious mood, less grimly cheerful and resolved
than they had been. The meeting with the Skraelings
had cracked their hard endurance. It promised an end
to the almost more-than-human efforts of the three
weeks since they had left Hóp, and yet it did not furnish
a clear objective. Were they even going in the right
direction? Would it not be better to abandon the heavy
boats, at least for the time being, and to set off in the
direction which the Skraelings had pointed out? Some

said one thing, and some another. Even those who held to continuing up the river were half-hearted. The current had become very swift and most of the time they were in the water, hauling the boats up slippery and shallow rapids over uneven footing. By night they had made little progress.

Paul said nothing until they had eaten. Then he held a council at which every man might speak his mind. But he spoke last.

"We came here by our boats and by our boats we must return when this adventure is over," he said, standing while the red light of the fire played upward upon his face and showed not his eyes but the hollows that held them. "We must not abandon our boats for any reason. We must follow the route of the Greenlanders. We have not found their boats; they must have gone up this river. If we should wander off unguided into the prairies, who knows what will-o'-the-wisp we might follow? Two or three men indeed might go with natives, but not the main body. To follow at the Greenlanders' backs may be the long way, but in the end it is the safe way."

Suddenly he gave the laugh which endeared him to his followers. "And just now," he added, "it is certainly the hard way. Yesterday while we camped, Johan and I followed up this river. In a little while it turns northeast in the wrong direction for us. I climbed a hill, and in the distance I could see forests and hills along to the east of us. Though the ground rises rapidly in places, the Greenlanders have made use of their rollers and taken their boats southeast uphill, apparently along a series of small lakes and carries toward the top of the divide. Perhaps after this is reached the streams will run easterly toward Vinland and our work grow easier.

But first we must climb steps of earth from pond to
pond.

"You have worked hard, but the work you have done
before will look like play to what lies ahead. Yet the
Greenlanders went up, with their women and children.
Do you think that you can do it?"

Eagerly Paul's hearers accepted the challenge, and
that night they slept deeply and at ease, their brief
uncertainty over. They were eager for the morning, so
that they might wrestle with their violent playfellow,
the river, and the long carries beyond.

"Put me at the bow of the leading boat, my Paul,"
begged Sira Andres, "and let Eirik be stationed at its
stern. You shall see how she shall swim and climb, like
a young seal. Then follow who can!"

"We will trace you by the snorting," answered Ulf,
who would jest with a priest as quickly as with any
other man, and in high good spirits they set out once
more to throw their strength against the strength of
this nameless land.

Chapter 15

The Picture Rock

IF THE GREENLANDERS had not been there before
them, Paul Knutson and his men might never have
reached the lake at the top of the height of land,
several hundred feet above the river. There were small
ponds to help them and streams which made dragging
and lifting the boats a little easier, but there were long
carries, all uphill, and only the knowledge that men and
women and children had been there earlier spurred on
the men to the work.

"They had a hundred men to every ten of us," grumbled Gunnulf during a rest, and Nicolas laughed at him.

"Yes, and ten boats to carry for every one of ours."

The King's Conscience looked like a death's-head these days. He staggered when he walked, but his thin bony hand dragged at the gunwale every time his boat was on the rollers. Sira Andres handled the bow of the leading boat and Eirik the stern. With priest and Lapp hauling and lifting tirelessly, struggling ahead, the others had to follow. A little above the river, they came into a belt of forest. Great trees these were, many of them as tall as a steeple and so large that four men had to join hands to make a belt around one. They were not pines, but had leaves of various shapes which made a pleasant shade overhead and sounded like running water along the boughs when a wind stirred them. The Scandinavians, struggling upward among their trunks, would often have found them barring the way, but here the earlier passage of the Greenlanders proved an enormous help. A road had been cleared through the smaller growth, overgrown a little now but easy to trace, and they had only to follow.

Johan Markusson never finished that journey. At one of the rests he said to Gunnulf:

"Here, friend, help me bind up my leg. Back a little way I heard a sharp rattling sound. I couldn't see what it was and paid little heed, for we had the boat on poles then, but something struck me on the left calf and there was a thick patterned serpent of some sort which had bitten me. I kicked it aside, but now my leg is swelling."

Gunnulf saw that Johan needed more help than he could give, and called Eirik, who cut and sucked the wound and laid wet clay on it. But he too had come too late.

Only Sira Andres was in time to hear Johan's confession and to prepare him for death before he became delirious. He died at dawn, and they buried him and put a cross at his head.

"It is strange," said Eirik after the short service at his grave. "Johan was a grumbler when things were easier with us. I have thought sometimes last winter that he might succeed in undermining everything which Paul was trying to build up. But see how hard it is to judge a man! Once the pinch came, he went with a light heart and a good word and died without complaining of his fate."

Olav felt a coldness at his heart.

"And here the poor man lies in a land without a name, killed by a creature without a name, under trees unlike any that we know."

"Are you not taught that he is in heaven?" Eirik asked. "What matter, then, where his body lies? The Norse have not been squeamish about such things, but have strewn their bodies like blowing leaves in a wind along all Ireland and England, the rivers of France and that fine island they call Sicily, let alone Iceland, Greenland and the Western Isles."

"Up, everyone!" came Paul's well-known shout. "It is still early. Let us see how far we can take the boats today."

At midmorning of the fifth day, after a last steep, heartbreaking struggle, they reached a larger lake at the top of the divide. From the high bank they looked down. It lay between its uneven shores, its tender blue reflecting the summer clouds. The great green trees above them made a canopy overhead, and not very far away a little island of rocks, like a stony snout, broke through the water. Its mated island, a few miles farther off, raised a small rocky head in answer. At their coming, a flock of ducks, which had been cruising the cove below

them, flew up, their wings whistling sweetly, and on
the island the men could see the ungainly black shapes
of cormorants sunning themselves with outstretched
wings after their morning's fishing.

That there were fish was not a matter of doubt. The
lake lay so still that they could see the slow rings forming every time a fish touched the surface where a moth
or fly struggled on the velvet skin of the water. After
so much labor, the place seemed like heaven itself, so
calm, so green and blue, so lost in a dream of clouds and
fair summer sky.

"Let us get the boats down to the shore," ordered
Paul. "Then we can come back and enjoy a well-
earned rest."

They used rollers again, holding the heavy boats back
with walrus hide thongs and blessing them because even
under the great strain they did not snap. The three
boats moored at last, the men's work was done. Like a
pack of schoolboys, they stripped off their clothes and
went swimming, challenging one another to racing
matches, and wrestling in the water to see who could
hold the other under and still keep his own head above.
Only Sira Andres, Paul and Nicolas, who sat propped
up against a tree apparently more dead than alive,
remained on shore near their weapons.

"For," as Paul said, "if the trees are pleasant for
shade, they are also excellent for ambush. When you
have done with your sport, we will clear out the underbrush around the fire."

But here, cool and slippery and at play, it was hard
to think of any danger. Olav remembered Ohenaw and
Shakaka with her copper cross and forgot the fort at
the bend of the river and the seventeen crosses burned

into the wood of the overturned boat not forty miles away. He forgot the nameless snake which had bitten Johan by the carry, and the weary dangerous months of voyaging which lay between him and Hestnaes. Laughing, challenging now one, now another, he grappled, held his breath, now went under, now came up again, broke free, returned to the attack, and at last, all sweat and weariness washed from him, returned with the others to dry himself, like the cormorants, before dressing.

But as he sat at ease on a rock among his friends, his feet still in the water, Olav happened to notice a rock with a flat surface which rose up out of the lake along the shore a little beyond them.

He called Eirik's attention to it.

"Are those not figures of some sort, Eirik?"

Eirik squinted. "Yes, something strange. I cannot quite see."

Ulf turned his falcon gaze upon the rock.

"I see hands printed red along the stone and those big deer with heavy horns and men with bows. I have once seen much the same in Norway scratched in the rock near the sea by people who, men say, lived there before our people."

"I shall swim over and look at it more closely," said Olav. "Who will come with me?"

Everyone was sleepy now, and unwilling to return to the cold crystal of the lake, so only Eirik came with him, and Smyrill, running along the shore abreast the swimmers. But Ulf and Benedikt stayed by the boats with their swords at hand in case the swimmers were attacked by a lake monster, as Ulf said, jesting. Or half-jesting, for here, where almost everything was strange,

they could not be sure what creatures they would find
by land or water, and there was no one to tell them
what to expect.

Olav and Eirik came upon nothing more terrifying
than a dark mother duck followed by seven half-grown
ducklings which had been feeding in a small cove between two boulders. They swam out in a flurry of
quackings and the swimmers laughed and let them go.

When they came to the flat-faced boulder with the
pictures on it, they lay in the water studying it for
some time. The upper part of the rock showed the
figures of half a dozen men. Two had bows in their
hands and one carried a hatchet, much too large. In
spite of their weapons, they seemed small and somehow
defenseless, these little outlines of people in such a
wide land. The deer, both horned males and their cows,
were scattered over a larger surface. The two men recognized the awkward shape and great horns of the animal,
which they had seen more than once. Beneath them
were the red imprints of many hands, some larger and
some smaller.

"See," said Olav pointing, "that man must have lost
his left thumb, and there is another without a finger."

"I do not like the color," said Eirik somberly. "You
would say that these hands had been wet with blood
when they were laid against the rock. Let us go back
to the others."

They had been in the water so long that by the time
Olav reached the place where the boats were moored
and had returned to his rock to dry, he was shivering
uncontrollably.

"What is the matter?" teased Benedikt. "Have you
seen a ghost, my Olav? Flail your arms against your
chest, and start the blood flowing again."

Eirik, whose body seldom showed anything, did not shiver, but he seemed abstracted and scarcely listened to what the others were saying.

All that day he remained wrapped in his own thoughts and remote. Even to Olav he had little to say. Paul, after setting lookouts, had decreed for the others a day of rest.

"Tomorrow we will go fishing and see what it is that noses up from the water," he said. "But this afternoon let us do nothing but be at our ease."

Everyone was glad to have a chance to be quiet. There was little laughter or talking. Some slept in the shade. Some mended or washed their clothes, some polished their weapons. Only Smyrill seemed restless, starting up, listening, scenting the wind, and then, as though he heard or smelled nothing after all, lying uneasily down again. When at last he went to sleep beside Olav, he lay twitching and whining.

Eirik broke a long silence. "Smyrill is having bad dreams. I wonder what they are? An animal feels the shadow of the future more quickly than a man."

"He is hungry," said Olav. "Probably he dreams that he is hunting."

"Perhaps," said Eirik, but it was clear that he had other thoughts.

A rustling wind, followed by another thunderstorm, came up late that afternoon and there were flashes of lightning and a crashing of thunder overhead for half an hour. The men rigged up a sail as a tent and sat looking out over a purple lake thatched with black riven clouds. Then as suddenly as it had come, the storm rolled eastward, leaving the west clear once more. The sun painted a tall rainbow on the dark vaporous east. Its pillars stood in the waters of the lake. The men could see the ripples through bright stripings, and higher up, there showed the faint lines of the trees on the opposite shore, washed in a jeweled light.

"Let us thank God that he has sent us to a land rich in beauty," said Nicolas, recovered somewhat from his earlier exhaustion. "See how the wings of that gull are dipped in glory!"

They went to bed early that night, Paul taking the first watch as lookout. Ever since finding the earth-works and the grave of the Greenlanders under the boat, he had established a night watch. The last thing that Olav saw before falling asleep was Paul's burly figure seated against a tree trunk, his face lighted by the red of the failing fire, his eyes gazing quietly off into the darkness of the trees, and his big head bent a little as though listening.

Chapter 16

The Excursion

THE MORNING dawned as calm and fair as the day before had been, and Olav woke refreshed and filled with a pleasant sense of anticipation. But Eirik was gloomy.

"I dreamed last night of an old man whom I used to know, who has long been dead. But last night he seemed alive and came to tell me certain things which I would rather not have heard just yet."

But when Olav asked him what the old man had said, Eirik became taciturn. "If he had wished to tell you, no doubt he would have come into your dream, too. He didn't, so it is none of your business."

Olav was used to these mysterious glooms of Eirik's and paid little attention to his surliness. The Lapp was like an old dog, faithful and trustworthy, which allows itself only at times to be patted. Now Eirik wished to be left alone. After breakfast he sat by himself, rewinding his fishing thongs and hooks about small flat pieces of clean wood.

Suddenly he drew his right hand away and looked at it. A hook had torn the flesh of his index finger and the blood was welling up from the small cut, slowly and darkly, as though some red underground spring had broken forth into the light. The drop grew larger and larger, hung, broke and ran in the smallest of scarlet rivulets across the finger and cascaded to the ground. Another followed and still another and another while Eirik brooded upon them.

"Let me bind it up," exclaimed Olav. "It is a small matter."

"A small matter," Eirik repeated, and then said again as though he did not know that he had spoken, "a small matter," but still he stared down at the pulsing spring of red blood on his finger end.

Paul appeared, vigorous and alert.

"Two boats for fishing, friends, and the other ten stay here with our things. Let me see, who's for the lake? Sira Andres, you certainly will still be in the bow of the first boat, as in the climb," and Paul named off seventeen men, Norwegians and Swedes, including Nicolas Byrgeson, who looked quite eager at thought of the expedition.

"One man more," he said. "Eirik, you must be in the stern of the first boat as Sira Andres must be in her bow. That completes the fishermen. Benedikt, you are in charge at camp. We will be back well before dark."

Paul turned to climb down the bank but Eirik detained him, holding him by a sleeve.

"Take the boy instead. A day's fishing means more to him than to me."

"Nonsense," said Paul. He could not allow the details of his plans to be changed, or there would be continual arguments. "He can come next time. Hurry up, Eirik. The others are all gone."

Eirik did not release Paul's sleeve.

"I have a pain about the back," he said. "I do not wish to sit all day in a boat."

"Then I will take Ulf."

Now the Lapp blocked Paul's path. He let go the sleeve he had held.

"Paul Knutson, have I asked any favor of you at any time?" he said, so low that his voice carried to no one but the man to whom he spoke.

Paul looked at him in surprise and shook his head.

"I ask you, now, if I have done my duty well, not to refuse."

Paul clapped him on the shoulder.

"What is all this talk about a little matter? I see that you are set on having your own way, Lapp. But no one can say that you have not earned a few favors. Stay here then. Olav," he shouted, "hurry up! You're going. And, yes, I suppose your Smyrill can come. If he doesn't sit still, we will heave him out, and he can wait for us on the shore."

Olav seldom went counter to Eirik's wishes—never on small matters—and he was glad enough to go fishing, since Eirik was in one of his ill-humors and did not wish to go. Smyrill at first seemed eager to get to the boat. Only when he saw that the third boat was not coming with the others, he whined and scratched at Olav's knee and thrust his head up into the boy's face as though trying to explain some uneasiness. Paul looked over his shoulder, frowning at the disturbance, and Olav sharply ordered Smyrill down. For some time the fishing took place near the first island and in sight of the ten men left behind, whom the fishermen could see lounging about on shore and at the camping place at the top of the bank.

"Don't go wandering off by yourselves!" Paul shouted once, as Ulf and a man named Haakon started off along the top of the bank away from the others, and they waved, to show that they had heard, and returned toward the fire.

The fishing was good. Small fish and large, they rose to the bait, and Nicolas caught an enormous pike which nearly pulled him over the gunwale before it was hauled in. Everyone wanted one like it. Sira Andres was the next to catch one, but he lost it just as it was half out of the water.

"Alas, God is punishing me for my gluttony!" he wailed. "As I saw that fish appear above the surface, my mouth watered with sinful greed."

As the fishing went on, everything else was forgotten. The men forgot where they were. So far as they were concerned, Bergen might have been just beyond the trees. Olav was not having much luck with the line which Eirik had given him. He alone seemed sad among the men laughing around him. He kept seeing Eirik's bleeding finger, and brushed the memory away from him. Why remember such a pinprick? Yet he remembered it. And there were the cormorants drying their wings. They seemed like devils giving a fiend's blessing from the rocks. And the fish flap-flapping at the bottom of the boat under his feet looked at him with round

desperate eyes. They were drowning in air; they were
dying, and there was no one to help them.

Secretly Olav leaned down, and, picking up one small
slippery, feebly struggling fish, put it over the side back
into the water. A moment later he found himself looking
defiantly into Paul's amused eyes and stifled an impulse
to explain.

All day Olav sat miserable, rowing when the others
rowed, fishing when they fished. The hours seemed endless. They had turned a point and were in another bay,
not far from the second island, for fish always bite
best near islands, the men said. There were more black
cormorants on this island too. When they flew up from
the rocks or water they beat their wings heavily and
circled low, as though they found it difficult to stay
aloft. They were like souls, Olav thought, heavy with
sin, which try to rise to God but are borne down again
by their own weight. He hated rocky islands because
they always reminded him of the battle in the Narrow
Straits. He looked at Paul. Was he too remembering
that Sigurd lay somewhere between such a skerry and
the shore? Often for days at a time he forgot that it
was Paul who had led that battle and who afterwards
had sealed the shame of Sigurd's memory by finding no
excuse for his friend.

Olav touched Ingrid's bracelet. It was a talisman
when his thoughts grew sad.

A little before midafternoon, Paul gave the order for
the return to camp. The two boats had recently fished
at some distance from one another, but now they went
down the lake, side by side, with a measured flash of
oars. A light haze had risen, which took the color out of
everything. The sun was silver, not gold; the water a

cold pale gray and the forest along the shore seemed dreary and monotonous. But the men were in good spirits. The fishing had been excellent, and now they sang one of the accustomed rowing songs, timing their strong strokes to its rhythm.

As they drew clear of the point, Olav looked over his shoulder toward the still distant camping place and felt an unexplained relief at seeing the smoke of the fire rising in a thin dissolving column above the trees. Eirik's ill mood had affected him, it seemed, and Smyrill had behaved uneasily all the day. Now the greyhound huddled in the bottom of the boat, shivering, and when they reached the shore he hung back, not leaping out over the gunwale as he usually did. Olav had to order him out and drag at his collar before he would come at all, and then he pushed against the boy's legs, nearly upsetting him.

"They must all have fallen asleep," said Paul, and then shouted, "Ho, men! Come help carry the fish!"

Paul waited a second, but there was no answer. His face changed, and dropping the two great pike he had hooked by the gills, he swiftly started climbing the steep bank. Olav followed, close at his heels, with Smyrill and the others as fast as they could come and all in silence.

The fire was still burning; the last wood must have been put on not much over an hour before. The ten men lay scattered about it, but not in sleep. In one thing they were alike: each man seemed wearing a scarlet hood of blood which ran down over his face. Even death in this land had a terrible new quality, as though these men had been killed by creatures not human.

Behind him, Olav could hear Sira Andres break the awful silence with loud prayer and some of the men joined in. But Olav did not heed their voices. There lay his Eirik with two arrows through his broad chest— Eirik, who had been like a foster father to him ever since he could remember. In this land beyond the world they had so often talked together of Sigurd and of Hestnaes and of the people there. Eirik was part of Olav's thought always; Eirik's wisdom had always been at his side.

And his love.

For Eirik had put on the terrible scarlet hood by his own choice. Gudrid had said in Greenland that of the four, three should wear it, and two against their wills, but Eirik had taken it on to save Olav, with his eyes opened by signs and dreams. Oh, Eirik, Eirik! There lay Benedikt, all in a heap, and Ulf still propped up by the tree against which he had set his back while life was in him.

"See," said Paul softly, "Ulf is smiling. He died fighting. There are bloodstains on the ground before him." But if the attackers had lost men, they had carried them away with them, as they had taken the swords and daggers and battle-axes of the men they had killed.

All this time Smyrill had been howling, but Olav had not heard his howls any more than he had heard Sira Andres' prayers. He looked at Ulf, who had been his friend, and at Benedikt, who was the kindliest courtier who had ever served a king. He looked at Eirik, who had died before he could draw a sword, shot down like a stag by the hunters. What harm had Eirik ever done these strangers that they should kill him?

Olav put dried meat in his pouch. He took a thong and tied it to Smyrill's collar and the dog stopped howling and looked up at him, eagerly. He went to Paul, where he knelt among the others.

"I am going," he told the man. "Wait a day before you bury them."

Paul stared fiercely into the boy's blind-looking dark eyes. If long ago at Bergen he had thought that Olav looked like a sleepwalker, now he seemed like one already dead, he was so utterly withdrawn. This was not a person who could be called back from what he was about to undertake, nor did Paul attempt it.

Instead, he rose to his feet and made the sign of the cross over Olav. Then he kissed him on each unheeding cheek, and said simply, "We shall pray for you."

Olav did not even speak again, nor so much as nod his head. With a last deep look at Eirik's face, he went to his own rolled-up sleeping robe, and took out from it his bow and arrows. He had worn his other weapons fishing, as had been the custom ever since they had found signs of fighting on the river.

Then he looked at Smyrill, and the dog whined eagerly and pulled away toward the northeast, his nose to the earth. One or two men made as though to follow him, but Paul called them back.

"There are too few of us," he said. "We can't let even revenge come between us and what we have set out to do."

"Then why did you let Olav go?" Gunnulf demanded hotly.

"Olav would not have obeyed me," Paul said. "He has gone mad. Did you not see his eyes? He is mad with grief and rage, and only his own death or the death of the Skraelings will heal him."

Chapter 17

Vengeance

THIS HOUR was Smyrill's. Now the tall greyhound went about his business with an animal
singleness of purpose that almost matched Olav's
own. No need to caution him to silence. Long ago
Smyrill had learned to make no sound while he hunted.
Nose to the leaves, still damp with yesterday's thunderstorm, he ran along invisible pathways, and Olav ran
behind him. In vain the last man among the marauders
had wiped out the trail as he went, brushing back the
bent twigs and straightening light stalks with the
stick he held in his hand. He had not guessed that
he had a dog to deal with. Perhaps he did not even

know that there were two boats out of sight behind the point of land. Who can tell how far they may have already come that day, before they noticed the smoke, and spying from the trees, saw strangers on their hunting grounds, and coolly killed them?

But if they thought all had been killed, they still did not assume it. Leaving dead men behind them, they were careful not to walk on a beaten trail. Yet to Smyrill's keen nose their path was clear enough. A mile and a half from the lake he drew to one side, whined, scratched a little. Olav, putting aside wet leaves, saw that the ground had been disturbed. He thought that three men had been buried here.

"Good," he said to Smyrill, "that is a beginning."

Once the others were lightened of the burden of their dead, they began to put more care into confusing the trail that they left. Smyrill again and again was forced to return on his tracks. Sometimes the Skraelings had made use of a ridge of rock; once they had walked for half a mile along a stream in the opposite direction from that which they had been following. Smyrill lost nearly an hour running up and down the banks before he picked up their scent again. But then he was off, nose to the ground, and Olav followed tirelessly.

It was growing darker in the woods. The summer nights came sooner now, and with the dusk, the thrushes began to sing, one answering another with slow, calm, gentle notes. Olav heard them, and at the same time did not hear them. His senses were alert to every sound and sight and odor in the forest, alert as they had never been before, but his spirit only took note of those things which fed its purpose, and the songs of the thrushes brushed past his ears as had the prayers of Sira Andres. Oh, Eirik, Eirik, Eirik!

Between the trees for a moment he saw the evening star. It burned so large and yellow that he knew the light haze must have dissolved again. That was good. A moon would be rising soon. He might need its torch, but now there was still a glimmering of daylight in the west, and the sky through the leaves was a soft blue, darkening all the time. Smyrill went on, a little faster than a walk, a little slower than a run. Although he made no sound, Olav, sensitive to his every breath, knew that the hound was on a warmer scent. They had begun the pursuit nearly five hours earlier, and in spite of losing time by the stream, they must have traveled much faster than those they followed, who had first been burdened by their dead, then had stopped to bury them, and after that had lost time in making false trails. Also, they may well have been tired from a long day's travel and it was likely that more than one was wounded, since three were dead.

As Olav felt Smyrill's excitement increase, he held him back by the collar, advancing cautiously. All might be ruined by flushing their enemy unexpectedly. With every step it seemed to grow darker. How could the thrushes go on singing? Smyrill strained at the collar, sprawled out, hugging the ground, his nose feeding upon the scent. His claws dug into the leaves, yet damp as they were, they gave no betraying rustle.

Olav leaned down, touching him with his left hand, whispering, "Quietly, Smyrill. Easy, boy, easy," and the dog responded a little to his master's will and pulled less frantically at the collar. Now Olav could scarcely see the ground. Smyrill, directly ahead of him, had become no more than a gray patch in the blackness, but still the thrushes sang on among the black boughs

overhead. This was no time nor place for their singing. Be still, birds. Oh, Eirik, Eirik!

A small red eye winked and went out. Now it winked
again, low to the ground. The trees were always
moving in between Olav and the eye, blotting it out,
but it always reappeared. So they had dared to build
a fire! That was good. He would be able to see better,
even by such a small red fire as this.

Now he leaned forward, folding his arms about
Smyrill. He could not whisper, but his arms said, "Be
still. It is not quite time," and Smyrill shivered with
impatience and stopped pulling at the thong. If they
had been silent before, they were much more silent
now, as they went off to one side a little way. Olav
found a fallen tree and sat down upon it, and in the
darkness shared the dried meat with Smyrill. He still
kept the thong wrapped three times around his hand,
but the hound seemed to understand, and sat at his
feet. They both ate, although both alike shook with
excitement.

At last the thrushes had become silent, but there
were other sounds of men moving about the fire and
now and then of someone speaking in a low guttural
voice. They too were eating, or so Olav judged. They
had camped near a stream, for Olav could hear it
trickle among small roots and stones, in a sound
almost as peaceful and gentle as the singing of the
thrushes had been. Then, as he listened, the noises of
the camp quieted, and only silence came from the men.

"They are tired," thought Olav, and he was glad,
for then they would sleep soon. This waiting was
exhausting, far more difficult than the trailing had been.
He was so eager to be at the business! But he was
cunning as any fox hunting partridges. And in his

case, all the odds were against him. He must not make the slightest mistake in his reckoning.

He waited, perhaps an hour, tense and still, so tense that when he got up at last he could scarcely walk. Pins and needles ran up his feet and into his legs, but after a few steps the blood returned and he was sure of his footing again. This time Smyrill did not tug at all. He walked shadowlike by Olav's side and the thong hung slack between them.

At the edge of the glade, Olav stopped again to reconnoiter. The fire still burned, but very low, and the Skraelings slept about it, their feet to its warmth, their heads in shadow. There was something weary about their pose, and perhaps a suggestion of pain. He counted five. This had been a small party, then, a war party of eight, perhaps. Had they left no lookout? Yes, there he was, standing, leaning against a tree trunk, and once again his pose suggested that he was weary and perhaps wounded, too. They had not killed the Norse wolf without feeling his fangs.

Olav felt Smyrill stir beside him, but a touch was enough. His eyes still were bent on the scene, and then he saw what he had been looking for. The lookout came forward into the circle of light and moved the ends of the firewood in toward the flame. His face was hideously striped with paint. Olav could not tell whether he was young or old, but thought that he was young. A flesh wound on his chest still bled a little as he moved.

Then he returned to his post by the tree.

But by the mended light of the fire, Olav had seen the hoops of green wood and what was drying upon them—light hair and dark. These were the trophies of his friends, of Ulf and Benedikt and of dark Eirik.

What need to wait after this? Would that there had
been twice six men so that he might more properly
avenge his own!

He tied Smyrill's thong to his belt and tested and
put an arrow to his bow. As he felt the feather of the
shaft beside his ear and the pull of the bow, strong
and tensely drawn in his other hand, all his sorrow left
him, and his heart was light and merry. Three arrows
he shot, one upon the heels of the other, and the
Skraeling watcher fell forward, making only a kind of
grunt. One sleeper woke and half sat up, and Olav put
an arrow through his body. This man gave a coughing
shout; little time remained now for preliminaries. Olav
shot once more at another body crawling away from
the light of the fire, and then throwing his bow to one
side and loosening Smyrill, he pulled free the sword
his grandfather had carried, and with his battle-ax in
his left hand, ran forward, shouting, and striking, with
Smyrill, no longer silent, beside him.

It was scarcely a fight there beside the fire, but a
taking of earned revenge. The three unwounded, or less
wounded men, were confused and not yet on their
feet. Smyrill's roaring charge was as bewildering to them
as Olav's weapons. Only one man fairly gained his feet
and his stone battle-ax, and Olav fought and killed
him with his sword. Another man from the ground
thrust a Norse knife into Olav's leg. He scarcely felt
the pain, then, as he turned to run him through.
Smyrill was holding the last man from escape into the
forest. He had gripped him by the legging from behind. The blows of the man's ax fell slanting. He could
not get free and Olav killed him there, ten feet from
the fire. He killed them all, quickly and joyously. Their

painted faces and slippery brown bodies did not seem like those of men.

Oh, Eirik, Eirik, are you happier now?

When he had finished, he took the things from the wooden hoop and very gently put them into his pouch, which would barely hold them all, but he would not carry them in anything of the Skraelings. Then he went to the stream and drank and Smyrill drank beside him. He washed the blood from his hands and body and from Smyrill and looked to both their wounds, the dog's first.

"Nothing so bad but that Eirik can tend to them," he thought, and then caught himself up, remembering that Eirik would never come to his aid again. But now the thought seemed like other sad thoughts, not like a fire in his brain. He felt very tired, but content. Eirik would not be buried unwhole, nor would he go to his grave unavenged. And Ulf, wild Ulf whom he had loved, and Benedikt, so courteous and careless in his ways! He had given them a friend's service. In heaven they would know what he had done.

The night was too dark, and he was too tired to return just yet. He lighted a dried branch at the Skraeling's fire and built another some way off, and he and Smyrill slept beside it, as well as they could for their stiffening wounds.

At dawn they drank again and returned along their trail, much more slowly now, limping and stiff, but yet in mutual good humor. They wasted no time now at the stream, and reached Cormorant Lake before noonday. Everyone except the two men on guard crowded about them, exclaiming and asking questions.

"Hold! Hold!" cried Paul. "Let him speak."

So with his hand on Smyrill's gray head, Olav gave a short account of the night's doings, praising the hound, but not himself at all. Then he gave Paul the pouch that held the strips which had been torn from the heads of their friends.

"Now we may bury them," he said. He paid no particular attention to Paul, and was surprised when Paul took him by the hand.

"Hold!" said Paul, again stilling the talk, and then went on. "The Lord has judged between us, Olav Sigurdson. Now before all men, I acknowledge that I wronged your father, Sigurd. Whatever in my blindness I thought, he died a brave man. Eirik the Lapp spoke the truth when he said that Sigurd's ship was coming to our defense, and I, who doubted it, proved but a poor friend. If you, Olav, can forgive the wrong I have done you and your father, we will return to your old betrothal with Ingrid, my only daughter and heir."

Olav glanced at the armlet he wore. Ingrid! There had never been a quarrel or misunderstanding between them. She had braved her father's anger in the king's house before all the court for his sake.

He scarcely knew how to answer Paul, for the old wrong had seemed for many weeks now something that had happened far away and long ago.

But he bowed, and thanked him and said that he was glad that Sigurd's name was cleared in the sight of one whom Sigurd had always loved before all other men, as he, Olav, valued Ingrid before all other women.

Paul again embraced him, but still he was not done with the matter.

"If I should die," he said to the others, "and if Olav, too, should die, and any of you get safely back to Norway, I lay it upon you to go to the king and

tell him what has taken place, that Sigurd's name may
be cleared before all men, by the judgment of God."

Once more and for a last time as they were eating,
Paul returned to the subject in talking to Olav.

"Eirik, God rest his soul, was angry with me because
I did not make this acknowledgment earlier, when you
saved my life at the hands of the northern Skraeling.
I think I wanted to, yet the proof was not quite clear
enough and perhaps I was ashamed to admit that I
was in the wrong. But this, Olav, was a true berserk
deed of yours. You left us a boy and came back a man."

The guard was changed, but Olav had no duties for
this day. He slept half the afternoon, tired out, but
later when the sun was low in the sky and the air was
cool and pleasant, Sira Andres wakened him. Eirik
and the others were to be buried. Now Olav could
join in the prayers and, for the first time, he wept.
Grief was no longer like a sharp knife cutting at his
heart, or a stone which he had swallowed and which
would kill him. The score had been settled. He could
breathe again, and speak and listen to what others said.

They had meant to drag the third boat up on the
shore and to leave it there, but in the end they
hauled and tugged and hoisted it up the steep high
bank and turned it over upon the grave, as the Greenlanders had done for their dead. These men whom they
were leaving in an unknown wilderness should have one
familiar object near them. Their hands, now dead, had
so very recently tugged at its oars, and hauled it
across the carries! It had been their constant care and
companion, along rivers, through lakes, up the shallow
streams. Now it should be a roof over their low heads
and surely they would rest more easily for its accustomed presence.

Chapter 18

The Rune Stone

AFTER a night's sleep, Olav and Smyrill were both very nearly themselves. This was indeed fortunate for Smyrill, at least, as Gunnulf and Thorvald took him along to guide them to the Skraeling camp where they went to bring back the best of the Norse weapons which the Skraelings had stolen. They returned in the early evening, heavily weighted down, and filled with praise for Olav's war skill.

The next morning Paul's voice again wakened the sleepers, and after a last prayer by the grave, they took to the two remaining boats and rowed away from the tragic spot. Even those who had lost no close

friend by that campfire felt the narrowing down of
their lives. The wilderness seemed to press upon them
more closely now that there were two boats instead
of three, and fewer voices raised in the stillness and
fewer shapes grouped about a fire by night.

Only one will remained, the will to find the Greenlanders before they died.

Their course lay as it had before, southeasterly, by
lakes and streams and carries, but there were no
heights to be climbed here and still the old trail of the
Western Settlement people beckoned them on farther
and farther from their distant base at Hóp. When it
was too late to return—and it was almost too late
now—would that overgrown trail disappear altogether,
leaving them stranded in the heart of this nameless,
beautiful land? For beautiful it still seemed to them
as the wild fowl flew up before them, and the fish came
eagerly to their hooks, and their boats came upon deer
sporting in the shallows. If there had been no Skraelings,
they could have loved this land, but now they felt
danger in every shadow.

Whenever possible, Paul chose an island for their
camp, or if there were no island, a hill. So they traveled
for five days and then they came to a small lake and
at the far end they found the Greenland boats. They
were pulled up on shore and covered over with old
boughs, leafless and brittle with years. No trail was
left leading away, and if there had been a sign or
message, it too had disappeared. They found several
broken arrowheads of flint: Skraelings had been here,
but when, it was impossible to say. There was a small
heap of bones, goats' bones from the skulls, but nothing
human and no sign of violence. But why had the
Greenlanders left their boats when the land was still

flecked everywhere to the southeast with lakes? And where had they gone?

There was a small hilly island in the lake and there Paul held a council. Nicolas sat on one side of him and Sira Andres on the other. The little Swede had not grown in beauty, but with his indomitable spirit he had taken on an added dignity, and his ragged cloak covered a body at last grown wiry and strong. Sira Andres had lost half his bulk, but not his fat man's laughter. Only Paul was little changed. His level eye, his quiet heartening voice were as they had always been.

"He is like the edge of the sword," Olav thought. "Without him, we should be but a blunt implement. A leader has to be many things besides a fighter."

They had need for wisdom now.

Paul spoke first.

"There are three courses open to us," he said. "We can abandon our boats, also, and remembering the Skraeling who wore a cross, start off toward the west in hopes of meeting with them again or with the Greenlanders. Or we can continue toward the east, in our boats, hoping to reach Leif's Houses and ultimately to be picked up there by Orm and Simon. Or, we can still return to Hóp. As you know, we have traveled upstream and uphill almost all the way. We should be able to make the return journey in about half the time. Sira Andres has kept count of the days, knotting each on a thong, and he believes that we are nearly ten days short of the Assumption of the Virgin. In that case, we should be able to reach Hóp before the river is frozen over. Each of these courses has its advantages and disadvantages. Let every man speak his mind."

Nicolas spoke first and shortly.

"There are no Greenlanders behind us. If they had continued toward Vinland, they would not have abandoned their boats. Then let us take to our feet and trust that God will guide us. There can be no turning back from his business."

"So say I," said Sira Andres.

Gunnulf's vote, too, was for the west and to leave the boats.

"We can but die," he said "and who values his life any longer?"

"I value my life still," Haakon, one of the Norwegian farmers, spoke up quickly. "I will risk it with any man for an object, but it is madness to wander off on foot into those plains as enormous as the skies."

"I hold with Haakon," said another voice.

"And I," said a third voice.

"And I," said a fourth. "If we are so eager to die, let us cut our throats here and have it over."

"Does no one speak for Leif's Houses?" asked Paul.

But no one wished to go to the uncertainties of Vinland through lands filled with new dangers. At least they knew the way to Hóp, and many wished to return there while there might still be time.

"We have done all we could," they argued. "The Greenlanders have vanished like birds which take wing and fly off into the sky. Then all that is left to the hunters is to go home."

"But birds settle again," Nicolas broke in fiercely. "The good hunter is not so easily discouraged."

"What do you say, Olav?" Paul asked.

"I think," said Olav, "that it is the part of wisdom to return to Hóp. But we have gone beyond wisdom now. Let us accept the great gamble of the plains."

A young man, Peters Haldorsson, who spoke little, broke out most unexpectedly now. "For my part, I should rather die on those great grassy meadows than live in any other land!"

"If we leave the boats, you are likely soon to have your wish, friend," said Haakon bitterly, but the votes were against him. Whether for love of Christ, or of the land, or because, their wills being fixed to one end, they could not turn back while there was still any hope at all of finding the Greenlanders, the larger number of men voted to leave the boats and to trust themselves to their feet and the westward course. But all knew that the chances of success were very small. Few of them would ever reach the boats again, if any at all, and then too late to return to Hóp, where the Knarr and their companions were waiting.

This was the end of the marked trail. They too would vanish like smoke dissolving in morning air. Each man felt as though he were already dead. He looked back on the long voyage and thought, "We have done well, but who will ever know of it?"

Paul, too, as so often, thought the thoughts of the others, even when they did not speak, but he translated their thoughts into action.

"We shall have to stay here for several days," he said. "While the rest of us hunt and fish for supplies to carry with us, would it not be well to leave an account of ourselves on some stone, Sira Andres? Olav will help you with the runes. I remember he once left a message in charcoal on a stone at Gardar. But this should be cut and cut deeply. Who knows? Someone of our race may follow us here, if not for five hundred years."

Everyone brightened at the idea. More than anything else the nameless anonymity of the land daunted
them, and the thought that their bones would probably
bleach among the grasses, no more regarded than any
beast's. The boat that they had left with its crosses
at Cormorant Lake would rot and fall slowly apart
and be blended with the earth which held its rowers, and
so would the Greenlanders' boat at the river bend, but a
good piece of stone would stand for a thousand years to
tell their story.

That very afternoon they chose a smooth, dark gray
rock, roughly oblong, a little less than a yard long,
and more than a foot wide. Haakon and one of his
friends, both men used to work in stone, spent some
time in improving its shape, making it like a Norse
gravestone with one end sharpened to hold it in the
earth.

Next day Sira Andres began his work with a chisel,
with Olav and Smyrill in close attendance. Paul left
them three men as a guard. No one ever quite relaxed
now, even on an island.

But Sira Andres sang hymns as he worked and the
chips flew smartly. Olav blew the fine gray dust out of
the runes and there were the words, beginning. He was
eager to try his hand, but Sira Andres was enjoying
himself so much that not until late in the afternoon
could he bear to lay down the chisel.

"See that you make the runes of the same size, my
Olav," he warned uneasily. "And notice the space I
have left between them. We want this to look well."

That night they threw a cloak over their work and
would let no one see it, but the next afternoon, when
the others returned, they had everything ready, with
the stone upright in its place. Olav had even picked

some yellow wands of flowers and laid them in a bright band of color beside the rock, thinking of Eirik and Benedikt and Ulf and the other seven men with whom he had worked and laughed and exchanged kindnesses.

"Of course, it's not quite like an inscription in Norway," Sira Andres said, hiding his pride. "We had little room for all we had to say. I left out some of the unimportant words, so as to get more in."

Paul read aloud the epitaph, for epitaph he and all the others felt it to be, changing his voice for the words he put in between the words that were on the stone.

"*We were* 8 Swedes and 22 Norwegians on *an* exploration journey from Vinland through the west. We had *a* camp by 2 islands one day's journey north from this stone. We were *out* and fished one day. After we came home *we* found 10 *of our* men red with blood and dead. Av*e* M*aria* save *us* from evil."

"Why do you say 'one day's journey'? It has taken us more nearly five to come here?" asked one of the men, a herdsman of Paul's, better with his hands than his head.

Paul was always patient with the man. "A 'day's journey' means a good day's sailing, Edvin. You have often heard us speak of that. It is twelve vika, as when on land we say twelve rests. Between one resting place and another, people reckon six miles or thereabouts."

The man nodded. "Twelve rests," he repeated. "Yes, that is more like it. Is Sira Andres going to say nothing of Orm and Simon and the men left at Hóp?"

"There is no more room," said Sira Andres, a little sharply. He was very proud of this inscription and did not welcome any criticism, especially from such a fellow as this Edvin. But Paul agreed with the man.

"We should all have a place on the stone," he

declared. "Couldn't you write something along the side, Sira Andres?"

"It would take another day," the priest grumbled.

"Then we shall wait another day," said Paul. "What is it that King David says? 'As for man, his days are as grass: as a flower of the field, so he flourisheth. For the wind passeth over it, and it is gone; and the place thereof shall know it no more.' So it may well be with us, but when we are gone this stone will remain. And a date, too, would be a good thing. It may be hundreds of years before it is read."

Sira Andres could not quite reconcile himself, even at Paul's suggestion, to make any additions to his work. Next day he allowed Olav to put the new writing along the side, entirely by himself. Now it was Olav who sang and whistled, eagerly cutting the lines into the hard stone, seeing Hóp and the wide estuary and the Knarr before his eyes as he worked, and imagining good Orm and the short one-eyed Greenlander, Simon, playing at chess in the hall of the great house, while the others watched them. He left out the "we" and "our party" which he thought would be understood, and even wrote "year" instead of "year of our Lord" as was more proper, but he was proud of his work, as Sira Andres had been of his. It took three lines, and his runes were as regular as the priest's.

"*We* have 10 of *our party* by the sea to look after our ship 14 days' journey from this island. Year 1362." Now everyone was well content. All had been said.

Paul lingered beside the stone with Sira Andres and Olav after the others had returned to the supper fire.

He nodded toward it, and said, more to himself than to them, "That may be the only tangible thing which we leave behind us, for all our effort, for all our endurance, for all the great things we have undertaken, and the wonderful things we have seen. And yet I have a feeling that nothing is lost. We have lived a saga, even though no one may ever write down our adventures. And a saga is a greater heritage than a city. Would the Greenlanders trade the memory of Leif's voyages for all the buildings of Gardar? When others come here—and who knows but that they may be people of our own race?—they will find this stone, and their hearts will be strengthened by our hearts' steadfastness. Young men will wonder about us, and wonder is a great teacher. This is a beautiful land, and we Norse have been the first white men to behold it."

No one had ever heard Paul speak like this. Now Olav knew that these were the thoughts behind his level gaze, his quiet speech. His was the well of strength to which they all turned when thirsty. Long ago he had forgiven him. Now at last he loved him.

But Sira Andres rebuked Paul. "You do not speak of God in all this vaunting, my son."

"God is behind and in everything. If I did not mention his name, it was because it sounded through all I said. All good work is the work of God."

Sira Andres was satisfied. Besides, he smelled the odor of roasting venison. When there was no food, he fasted without complaint. But when there was meat, he ate until he could eat no more.

"Let us join the others. It grows late," he said and without waiting for his companions, lumbered off down the hill toward the fire by the shore.

Smyrill began suddenly to bark. He was usually a silent dog, but now he barked excitedly, not in anger, but in astonishment, perplexity and welcome, running a short way, then tearing back to paw at Olav's knee, and then running off again, and all the time barking.

It was quite late and the shores of the pond opposite the island were shadowy and indistinct under the trees. Paul and Olav could see nothing moving there, but Smyrill continued his wild barking and the low hills, back from the water, echoed the sound until it seemed as though a whole pack of greyhounds were giving tongue.

"Hush," said Olav, but Paul put a hand on his arm.

"Do not stop him. This has some meaning. See, he keeps looking toward where the Greenlanders' boats are beached. Someone must be there."

Chapter 19

"It Is Time for You to Depart"

SOMEONE *was* there at the shore. As Paul and Olav
listened, a shout came from the shadow of the
trees, but they could make out nothing clearly,
until Olav had silenced the half-frantic Smyrill.

Then they heard the words: "Ho, Norsemen! Send
over a boat to us!"

"Now praise be to God," said Paul, dropping to his
knees. "That is true Greenland speech."

When they reached the campfire they found that the
others had also heard the voice and had already un-
moored one boat and were tumbling into it. Everyone
wanted to go, but Paul, laughing, chose his crew.

"Sira Andres, yes, and Nicolas and Olav, but leave that yelping dog behind, and two more to help with the rowing. We don't know how many there are of them to come back."

"Are you not afraid of an ambush?" one of the men jested.

"Not after that Norse hail! Push off, we must not keep them waiting."

Olav sat beside Nicolas Byrgeson, down whose thin cheeks tears of joy were running. He was choking over the prayers of thanksgiving which tumbled from his lips. "Now let Thy servant depart in peace," he kept repeating.

As for Smyrill, he was not to be left behind. Ordinarily not fond of the water, this evening he plunged in after the boat, striking out with his long legs and arriving in time to wet everyone as he shook himself. But it was a moment for wonders and Smyrill's swim was the least of them. There was truly a Greenlander on the shore, a short strong figure of a man with fair hair, so much they could see even in the dusk as they fell upon him, embracing him, clapping him on the shoulders, striking hands with him, laughing through unashamed tears, while Smyrill leaped upon him with the same joy, dampening his leather shirt and leggings with his wet paws.

At last they led the stranger to the boat and with him his companions, who were all Skraelings, four young men and a woman. A voice he had heard before said to Olav, "Greetings, friend." It was Shakaka. When he had seen her last he had been with Eirik and Ulf and Benedikt. He felt again that sharp pang which often came to him when least expected. He was alive, and they were dead. But now this Greenlander had come, the circle was complete. The thing was finished and his friends had not died uselessly on a useless voyage.

Paul insisted that before they talked, the newcomers must eat, but as soon as it was possible, there was talk.

"My name is Thorfinn Sokkeson," the stranger began. "When the two Mandans came and showed us the armlet and its message, it was decided that I should come with them to the Place of Boats, and if I had not found you here I should, after a few days, have gone to look for you."

He paused for a moment and in that moment Gunnulf asked, "My cousin Margret, daughter of Haftor, is she alive and is she married?"

Thorfinn peered at the speaker across the fire and his eyes were laughing.

"Oh, so the Norwegian cousin is here? Yes, Margret is alive. Her father died and her mother made her marry, but it was against her will, and the young man was killed last year in a fight with a bear which he had wounded. She has always insisted that some day her betrothed would come, and here you are and a fine big fellow, I see."

"But what about the Western Settlement farm you were going to have?"

"Perhaps I shall have a finer one here."

"Good, Gunnulf. I am glad your affairs flourish," broke in Paul. "But let Margret wait for a while. Tell us, Thorfinn, why you left Hóp, where we had expected to find you, and why you went up the river and above all, why you left the boats here?"

"And I must know who you are and for what reason you have followed us to this land beyond the world," Thorfinn replied.

Nicholas broke in, "And tell us of your priest, and how it is with your souls, for it was because of the idolatry among you that Magnus Eirikson sent us in the royal Knarr to lead you back to the faith."

Thorfinn's face turned grave at these last words.

"We have already been led back, I believe. Somehow in Greenland the old gods seemed always near and too often our women said the old charms at the butter-making and now and then we ate horsemeat, in honor of Thor, and too many of our children bore such names as mine. But it was all foolishness, and was washed from us in the cold sea before ever we reached Hóp. In our troubles we turned only to Christ. We lost five boats and their people on that voyage. And at Hóp a sickness came. We did not prosper. At last we decided to seek Vinland, and it seemed easier to keep to the river, where we could meet with no storms. We killed the last of our cattle and sheep to make more room in the boats, but we took with us a few goats, hoping that when we reached Vinland they might multiply. We had the last still with us here, but did not delay the over-land journey by trying to take them farther. As you must have seen at a bend of the river, Skraelings fell upon us, and we drove them off, but we lost seventeen of our people. The Skraelings were a hunting party. Finding how many of us there were, they left us and went on toward the plains to kill the humped cattle and dry the meat. Now we know that they were Ojibwas, but then we had only one name for all the people of this country."

"Such a party killed ten of our men at the campfire, and Olav here followed them and killed every man."

"They too must have been Ojibwas. This rich land has for a long time been a battleground. The Mandans—

these people with me—hold it from their ancestors, but the Ojibwas have for years now been trying to drive them away from these lakes and forests. At last the Mandans have decided to go, and we have built villages together many days to the west, by a river, and only return here occasionally and are swiftly gone again."

"How does it happen that you have thrown in your lot with Skraelings?" Paul demanded almost sternly, and he stared at the five figures seated without motion behind the Greenlander.

Thorfinn felt the challenge in the other man's voice.

"It began in two ways. As we passed through those plains and came to the forest with such trees as we had never dreamed of, we began to love this land. Remember, we have known nothing but the ice and the little fields along the more barren fiords of Greenland. But it was strange to us. We knew no way to enter into it."

He paused, thinking of words to explain his meaning better and Olav said, "Nothing had a name."

"Yes," said Thorfinn, "that was it. Nothing had a name. Then on the bank of a stream we came upon a young Skraeling. He was badly wounded and delirious and had come to the water to drink. To us, all Skraelings were alike, and we would have killed him, but our priest and some of the women had pity on him and they took him in a boat and tended him. It was a long time before he was well and by then he had learned something of our speech. He taught us the difference between the Ojibwas and the Mandans, and hunted for us, and kept guard of our camping places and told us the names and habits of things and drew us maps of the country on the beaches, making the lakes clear and sticking in twigs for forests and piling pebbles to show us the height of the hills. We grew fond of him, but more than that, he opened the country to us. He was the doorway through which we passed into feeling at home in the land."

He looked at Olav and smiled.

"He knew the names of things."

"A pagan!" objected Nicolas.

"No, not even a pagan," said the other. "Our priest taught him our faith and he was glad to be baptized. Then he brought us news that his people had been again attacked and their villages destroyed. The remnants had gathered here and were holding a great council. We joined with them and they welcomed us. They saw our swords and battle-axes and our bows and begged us to go with them to fight the Ojibwas, but that we would not do.

" 'If you do not, they will kill you all, ambush by ambush, as you pass eastward through their country,' they told us.

"Then they asked if we would go westward with them into the plains. We had seen the plains, so endless, and the dark herds of humped cattle and the antelopes and the yellow flowers. So much earth! What could we hope for half so rich in Vinland? And we had lost so many of our people already.

"So after talking for days, we decided to go west with the Mandans. You should see our villages! The houses are like our round houses at home with bedsteads and a high seat between them and benches by the wall. We raise a yellow grain they have, whose ear is as long as a man's hand and very good to eat roasted or to grind into flour. Other things, too, we grow, round, some green, some yellow, and beans on vines and the hunting is good. And our women pick berries. The Mandans are quick to learn our ways and we theirs, as you see"—he pointed to the deerskin clothes that he wore. "Our women have tried spinning the underwool of the humped cattle, but so far the cloth they have made is harsh, far less comfortable than this to wear."

"But are they Christians?" Nicolas demanded in his high voice.

"Little by little," said Thorfinn. "They have all been baptized, but of course many scarcely speak our tongue and we still speak theirs imperfectly. But they are docile and eager to learn. The chief obstacle is that our priest, who understood them best, died last winter of a sickness."

"I will take his place." Sira Andres' voice boomed up from the shadows. "God's work must not fail for lack of servants."

"Wait," commanded Paul. "Thorfinn, will you not return with us? Are none of you tired of a land so far from home?"

The Greenlander shook his head.

"Sir," he replied, "we talked long of this when Shakaka brought the armlet. But no one wished to go back. Even the women wish to stay. And I think the reason is that our children are growing so tall and fair. You know that we who were raised in Greenland are a dwarfish lot, but now we have tall sons."

"Then, as I said, I will return with you," repeated Sira Andres. "I am not so lazy as I look, Thorfinn. You will find that I shall labor well in the vineyard with God's help."

"And I shall go to find this Margret," said Gunnulf.

"The last ale was drunk at Hóp," said Paul. "We will not be there at the wedding."

"But there will be no lack of wedding guests," spoke up Thorfinn. "You will be very welcome to us, young man. Though the priest is the greatest bounty of all."

"If Paul can spare me, I should like to join my lot to the Greenlanders," said Peters Haldorsson, who had once spoken in praise of the plains.

Nicolas hesitated, but his place was with the king. Besides, he had much to report to Magnus if he ever got back alive to Bergen.

"But let me have the woman's cross of copper," he begged Thorfinn. "No gift could I bring Magnus Eirikson so valuable as a cross worn by one who had been born a heathen Skraeling. If she will let me have it, she shall have mine in return," and he eagerly took from his neck a heavy gold chain on which hung a gold cross set with sapphires and uncut emeralds which the king had given him.

When Shakaka, at a few words from Thorfinn, took the thong from her neck and gave Nicolas her cross, he handed his to her, and then kissed the crude copper thing which he held, very reverently, before putting it on. His long intense mission was accomplished. They had found the Greenlanders and found them to be Christian and to make assurance doubly sure, a Norse priest was returning with them. Now Nicolas prayed that he might live long enough to reach Norway.

The same thought was in every mind. Each was thinking of his own hearth. Olav thought of Ingrid. She would be nearly twenty years old before he could hope to see her again—in two years, if they were lucky. In his mind's eye he saw her at Hestnaes, and he would tell her of all these things as she and his mother sat by the fire of an evening, their tall carved spindles in their hands, busily feeding out the weighted thread as they listened. And, please God, Smyrill would lie at his feet as he talked, for although Smyrill had welcomed Thorfinn so eagerly as something out of a lost past, the man was not his master nor did Smyrill wish to follow him.

They talked all night until the dawn, exchanging a thousand details of their experiences. Then Thorfinn at last rose and thanked Paul and the others for the long journey which they had undertaken for the sake of the Western Settlement.

"We left a message at the shore when we first left," he explained, "but, as you guessed, it was on wood and must have been taken. Tell our friends of the Eastern Settlement that we are well and content in our villages. I must start soon with the woman and the three Norsemen who have chosen to come with me, for the forests here are not safe for a small party. The four young Mandan men will go with you as hunters, but above all as scouts, until you reach the borders of the forest and the river whose waters are red. From there on you will be safe from the Ojibwas, and they will return to us across the plains."

The farewell was not an easy one for any of them. Fat Sira Andres they loved as a father, and Gunnulf and Peters were men well liked by the others. What was this flat world of plains and endless sky to which they were going, these farms whose cattle were humped and wild and whose produce was in grains and vegetables of which they had never before heard? And good Thorfinn who had left his ease and safety to come to them! And the gentle brown Mandan woman, Shakaka!

When the door of the forest closed behind them, they would be utterly gone from all human knowledge.

But for them was the return, Hóp, and beyond a winter at Hóp, the cold northern seas, and at last the Eastern Settlement where they must winter once more, before the Knarr might point her high dragon's head toward Norway and home. But now the whole way was known to them. Every river would help them, every hillside slant them toward the north. They left their dead behind them, but not unavenged. Their bones, Norwegian and Swedish alike, would guard the land until their people should come again down the lakes and across the carries. Paul Knutson's mission had been accomplished, and now Olav could think of Ingrid's welcome.

Sira Andres blessed them for a last time and prepared to get into the boat. The sky now was palest blue with the fire of the new-risen sun along the east, and a faint wraith of mist veiled the surface of the lake.

"What is the woman singing?" Olav asked Thorfinn in a low voice.

"It is the women's farewell to the warriors," Thorfinn told him. "They always sing it when the men start out.

> " *'Come,*
> *It is time for you to depart.*
> *We are going on a long journey.'* "

Paul gave the order and the boat pushed out from the island shore, with four rowers who would bring it back. But even after Thorfinn and the others had called their last farewells from the farther shore, and had disappeared from view among the trees, Olav stood

Afterword

Fifty years ago a Minnesota farmer named Olaf Ohman, in grubbing up an aspen tree on a rocky hillock near the town of Kensington, found a stone clutched in its roots. It was his son, a boy of ten, whose attention was caught by its tombstone shape, and who brushed it off with his cap and so found curious scratches along two of its surfaces. The authorities of the period doubted the authenticity of the inscription and for ten years and more the slab was used as a flagstone in the man's muddy barnyard, until a scholar, Hjalmar R. Holand, born in Norway, became interested in it. He has spent thirty years in studying the inscription, taking it to twenty-three European universities and finding parallels to nearly every rune in fourteenth-century usage. Even he could not explain why Norwegians and Swedes might share in such an expedition, until twenty years ago King Magnus Eirikson's original letter of authorization to Paul Knutson was discovered in the royal library at Copenhagen.

From the stone—now at the Smithsonian Institution in Washington—and the Magnus Eirikson Commission, and the known fact that the people of the smaller of the two Greenland settlements had about this time disappeared from their farms, leaving no trace behind them, and from various mooring stones, fire steels, swords and halberds of mediæval Scandinavian design found along the streams and lakes of Minnesota, Mr. Holand has constructed a fascinating theory, quoting authorities at every point. This I have in general followed, as well as his suggestion that some of the Scandinavians may have joined with the Mandans, an Indian tribe, which many of the first explorers found to be brown-haired, with gray or blue eyes, and famed for their gentleness and courtesy, living in houses very like the round form of the simpler Scandinavian houses.

Pierre La Verendrye, the first to visit them, as early as 1732, was told by the more easterly Indians that a race of whites lived to the west. He found these people not to be whites, but far more civilized than any of the tribes about them, and brought back from their country a small stone, apparently covered with runes, which he discovered set in a pillar near one of their villages, and sent to Paris, where, alas! it disappeared.

In 1832 the artist George Catlin lived for several months with them.

"I am convinced," he wrote, "that they sprang from some other origin than that of other North American tribes, or that they are an amalgam of natives with some civilized race . . . amongst the women particularly, there are many whose skins are almost white, with the most pleasing symmetry and proportion of features; with hazel, with gray, and with blue eyes . . . with mildness and sweetness of expression, and excessive modesty of demeanor, which render them exceedingly pleasing and beautiful . . ."

Their religion, too, seemed to have been derived from Christianity.

If one mystery is the disappearance of an entire

colony of eight or nine hundred people from Greenland without sign of violence (as the Norwegian priest, Ivar Bardson, recorded, who visited the scene while the cattle and sheep still grazed about the empty buildings); and the presence of a stone marked 1362 in the very heart of our own country is another; the origin of the Mandans is still a third, and that perhaps as unanswerable as the others, for five or six years after Catlin's visit smallpox wiped out "the kind and gentlemanly Mandans."

Here were three mysteries then, each as fascinating as the other, and possibly all connected. I have in the main followed Mr. Holand's theory which he so ably presents and defends in *Westward from Vinland* and *America 1355–1364*, but I have made a few changes. I have taken the liberty of having Magnus Eirikson sign his authorization in the spring of 1360 instead of during the fall of 1354, as I could not send Olav out on so long an expedition. Then, when Mr. Holand conjectures that we are to understand in the Kensington stone inscription "[we are] 8 Swedes and 22 Norwegians, I have conjectured "[we *were*]" largely because it was more convenient to deal with a smaller group. Where I have taken most liberties with Mr. Holand's theory, however, is in refusing to dismiss the lost Western Settlement as briefly as he does. Once having used their disappearance as a lever with which to arouse the king's crusading spirit, he brushes them aside, and assumes that Paul Knutson's expedition came upon no trace of them and turned from a search into an exploration. I prefer to believe that the Greenlanders *did* leave traces, and that Paul Knutson followed them into the interior, and that it was their far larger group which amalgamated with the Mandans. Again,

Mr. Holand believes it likely that only the men left with the Knarr got back to Bergen, but I, leaving the Greenlanders to settle down among the Mandans, bring Paul himself, Olav and the rest safely home. Nor is there any historical evidence against this possibility.

A book by Edward Reman, an experienced navigator, appeared in 1949, locating the places visited by the Norse in the various sagas. He places Karlsefni's Hóp, not in Leif Eirikson's Vinland, but at the mouth of the Nelson River, an added reason why the Green-landers—and so, Paul Knutson—might have gone there.

For some knowledge of Norway, I was fortunate in having Sigrid Undset's work, at once so scholarly and so alive. Her masterpiece, *Kristin Lavransdatter*, was laid during the reign of Magnus Eirikson.

A small book called *Viking Settlers in Greenland*, by the Danish scholar, Paul Norlund, was my authority on Greenland. Within its 155 pages a tremendous romance is compressed—the coming and complete disappearance of the Vikings, who for five hundred years clung to the green strips of land along the fiords, and then vanished, the Eastern as well as the Western Settlement, leaving the ruins of their churches and farmsteads behind them. The writer has spent summers in Greenland, excavating the frozen graves near Cape Farewell, and the heaps which hide the foundations of farms all along the lower western coast. His photographs show fiords and rivers, the walrus herds and the spindle whorls of the women. He answers almost every question that one could ask, except the last question of all, "When and how did they disappear?"

I read the Greenland and Iceland sagas for their matter-of-fact courage, and the curiously modern and vivid quality of the conversations. From the two volumes of Paul Du Chaillu's *The Viking Age* I took the riddles and the wonderful passage from the Rune Song of Odin, which Gudrid—who appears in the sagas, catskin gloves and all—chanted when she was calling up her spirits.

I happened to have a good deal of Eskimo material about the house in government pamphlets and books of travel. The most detailed and interesting of these was an old collection called *The Polar and Tropical Worlds*, lent to me by a neighbor. Actually I could use little of it, for Paul stayed among the Eskimos for so short a time.

Once traveling up the Nelson, my chief dependence was again upon Mr. Holand, but from the Jaques's *Canoe Country* I had a description of the painted rock, and from *Minnesota*, in the American Guide Series, I learned what kind of forest the expedition entered, upon leaving the Buffalo River, and what tribes of Indians they might have met with. In its pages appeared the little haunting song of farewell, not unlike the one sung today, "Now Is the Hour," but with even more left to be understood.

Twice the American Museum of Natural History kindly came to my aid, once in regard to the possible affinities between the Eskimo and Lapp tongues, and once to tell me what types of trees would have been found along the Nelson River and Lake Winnipeg.

Gerard Brett, of the Royal Ontario Museum of Archeology, gave me the exact wording of the labels of the Viking swords mentioned later.

As for spelling, I found every Norse name spelled in two and sometimes three different ways and chose the ones I liked best.

There is an argument which has never been settled as to whether or not the Indians learned their habit of scalping dead enemies from the whites. Many authorities believe the custom to have been indigenous, and, as the wording of the Kensington Stone seems to suggest that the ten murdered men had been scalped, I have assumed that such was the case.

During the hours when I have been at work, my thoughts have often gone back to something which my husband and I saw some years ago at the Royal Ontario Museum of Archeology in Toronto, which stirred my imagination as nothing else in a museum has ever done.

Near the entrance of one of the large rooms was a glass case in which lay three swords, their blades somewhat rusted, but still clearly outlined. Hilt and blade, the weapons were very similar.

On one card was printed: "Viking sword, 10th century, dredged from the Thames at London."

On the second card was printed: "Viking sword, 10th century, said to have been found in the Seine River (France)."

The third read: "Viking sword, said to have been found near Beardmore, Ontario, beside the Blackwater River, and close to Lake Nipigon."

We have only begun to read the early and hidden history of our land.